We turned and tried the d̶o̶
We heard screeching brakes a̶n̶d̶ ̶a̶ ̶c̶a̶r̶ ̶s̶k̶i̶d̶d̶e̶d̶ ̶t̶o̶
a stop behind us. I guessed it was the police, but
I couldn't have been more wrong.

The driver and passenger got out. Both wore
dark clothes; one was thin and weedy, one fat.
The thin one spoke. 'Robert and Lisa?'

Straight away I knew that these were the men
from the lifeboat.

'Is this them?' asked the other one. It was Mr
Potato. No doubt about it. He looked as stupid as
he sounded. In fact his face looked just like a big
spud. But stupid or not, he could hurt us, and
when he grabbed for us we ran.

The thin one tried to catch Lisa. She kicked him
hard where it hurts. He swore and doubled up.

Mr Potato threw himself at me but I ducked and
he fell heavily, right in the middle of a puddle.

'Run for it, Lisa!' I shouted.

We ran – ran for our lives . . .

Also available by Mike Smit,
and published by Corgi Yearling:

KNOT AGAIN!

Mike Smit...

ALL TIED UP

Very Strong String

Illustrated by
George Hollingworth

Whitby

CORGI YEARLING BOOKS

ALL TIED UP
A CORGI YEARLING BOOK : 0 440 86372 4

First publication in Great Britain

PRINTING HISTORY
Corgi Yearling edition published 1998
3 5 7 9 10 8 6 4 2

Copyright © Mike Smit 1998
Illustrations copyright © George Hollingworth 1998

The right of Mike Smit to be identified as the author of this work
has been asserted in accordance with the Copyright, Designs
and Patents Act 1988

Set in Century Schoolbook by
Phoenix Typesetting, Ilkley, West Yorkshire

Corgi Yearling Books are published by Transworld Publishers,
61–63 Uxbridge Road, Ealing, London W5 5SA,
a division of The Random House Group Ltd,
in Australia by Random House Australia (Pty) Ltd,
20 Alfred Street, Milsons Point, NSW 2061, Australia,
in New Zealand by Random House New Zealand Ltd,
18 Poland Road, Glenfield, Auckland 10, New Zealand
and in South Africa by Random House (Pty) Ltd,
Endulini, 5a Jubilee Road, Parktown 2193, South Africa

Printed and bound in Great Britain by
Cox & Wyman Ltd, Reading, Berkshire

To Shirleyann

1. The Holiday

I've spent my life wanting an adventure. Kids in books are always having adventures and solving mysteries. The Famous Five had about a hundred just to themselves. It's not right. They met smugglers, found treasure, met more smugglers, found more treasure. Even their dog Timmy had more excitement than me. If he was given a tin of Doggychops there would be a treasure map inside it.

But me? Nothing.

That is, until we went on holiday to Whitby. Then I had an adventure to end all adventures. An adventure that made me wish I'd kept my big mouth shut about wanting an adventure . . .

My name is Robert String. Yes, I know: 'That's *knot* a good name', and 'Are you going to be Robert *Rope* when you grow up?' I've heard all the jokes.

I blame my dad, Matthew. He gave me the name – I didn't choose it. He says I should be proud of the name as it's very old: 'You come from a long string of Strings!'

Very funny, Dad! He's a teacher, but other than that he's OK. Except he makes terrible jokes. I've a mum, Louise, and a younger sister called Rachael.

The story I'm going to tell you happened to me. I've tried to tell it just as I remember it. So let's get started.

I came in from school one afternoon and Mum said, 'We're going to Whitby this summer holiday.'

I was so excited I nearly fell asleep for a hundred years. But to be on the safe side I said, 'Oh, good.'

My friends all go to Disneyland in Paris or Florida or on safari in Africa. We were going to Whitby. I hadn't been so excited since Aunty

Beryl, Mum's sister, bought me a bobble hat for Christmas three years ago.

Even though I'd said 'Oh, good' in my most realistic voice, my mum said, 'What's wrong with Whitby? You know your dad and I love Whitby. If it wasn't for my job you wouldn't be able to have a holiday at all!' My mum works part-time in a school helping with some special needs children.

'I like Whitby,' I said, but by then I knew it was too late and I would be in for the 'You ungrateful boy . . . you don't know when you're well off . . . your father and I never had holidays until we were ninety' routine.

I stood there, nodding every now and then but letting her words go over the top of my head. It was only when Mum said, '. . . Robert, do you?' that I started listening again. Now I was for it. If I admitted I hadn't been listening I would be in trouble. If I tried to guess what 'Robert, do you?' was about and got it wrong it could be even worse. What if Mum had said, 'Do you want to start taking ballet lessons?' or 'Do you want Eric Pegg (the world's biggest twit who also happens to be in my class) round for tea?' I'd never live it down.

I decided to use that special word 'Yehno'.

You had to say it in a real mumble and with luck it could mean 'yes' or 'no' depending on the circumstances. I had invented this word especially for times like these. So here goes: 'Yehno.'

Mum looked at me as if *she* didn't know what *I* was talking about. That made two of us! But from the look on her face I could see that my scheme had failed and I was just about to have my ears bent inside out again. I'd probably be grounded for a year as well! There was only one solution.

'Oh, my leg!' I grabbed my leg and collapsed on the ground in agony. It was brilliant acting, better than the footballers I'd seen on telly. I writhed around. 'Oh, ow, eeh!!' Any second now Mum would do her Florence Nightingale impersonation, bandage my leg, kiss it better, give me a sweet—

'Get up, Robert, and stop being stupid!'

'But, Mum, my leg – I think it's broken.'

'If you don't get up and stop messing about making my floor dirty, it won't be a broken leg you're worried about.'

I stood up. 'Mum, it's a miracle – I'm cured – hallelujah!'

The only thing Mum hates to do when she's cross with me is smile or burst out laughing halfway through. It spoils the effect. I think she was going to laugh now because she coughed and very quietly said, 'Get out of my sight. Go on.'

I didn't stay to argue. I just left very quickly and ran out into the garden – both legs working perfectly.

Rachael was upside down again. She's mad on gym. Well, she's just mad really. She was doing a bridge, so I went over and stood in front of her. 'Oh, look. Dad's put a bench in the garden. I'll just sit on it.' And I pretended to sit on Rachael's upturned stomach. Of course she collapsed. Come to think of it, just as she would have done if she *had* been a bench Dad had put up.

Rachael shot off doing a series of forward rolls. I can't remember the last time I saw her walking properly. Perhaps she can't! Maybe she's got some dreadful disease – gymnitus – which means she can only move around using gymnastics. Poor Rachael.

I got my football out from its top security store – under a bush – and started kicking it about. I was Manchester United and was playing my dad's team – Barnet. There was no-one on his team and so the final score, 27–0 to Manchester United, was probably very realistic for a five-minute game.

I sat down on the pitch and pulled at the grass while thinking of how it might actually be quite good fun at Whitby. We went there a lot. Our holiday was only three weeks away and, if the truth be known, I couldn't wait.

2. Breakdown

The car journey from our house to Whitby was terrible. Mum and Dad were playing awful music from the Sixties and my personal stereo only had one speaker working. I think that's because when I got it out of my bag it looked as though somebody had tried to knit the wire into a hat. It doesn't matter how tidily I put it away – it always manages to knot itself into about a hundred knots. When I tried to untangle it I unknotted the wrong end and it made even more knots. In the end I got cross and yanked it and a green wire came out of one of the speakers. I pushed it back in again but I knew it wouldn't work and it didn't.

After ten minutes Dad wanted a mint, which meant we all got one. Everybody else always seems to have mints that last for ages, but no matter how hard I try I always bite mine by mistake and end up swallowing it and wanting another. I had to wait for Dad to want another one, or for Mum to decide it was time for another. I could really do with a giant sack full of mints – that way I might just have enough to last the journey.

Then, of course, I needed the toilet. Now if Mum or Dad need the toilet it's nature. If Rachael needs the toilet it's because she's young. If *I* need the toilet it's because I've deliberately set out to ruin the journey and give Dad a heart attack and a nervous breakdown at the same time. I'd been to the toilet before we set off, and had only sipped enough water to make sure I didn't drop dead, but now I felt as if I'd drunk a swimming pool. I felt sure something inside me would burst. Really Dad should have been pleased that I didn't want to explode over his precious car, but when I casually mentioned that I might need a toilet or even a bush in the next hour or so, you'd think I had threatened to throw Rachael out of the window. If Dad had been in a cartoon, he would have had smoke coming out of his ears!

Mum tried to make the peace. She told me to suck it in, tie a knot in it and then try thinking of something else. Rachael started singing 'The Water of Life' and I hit her, so Dad shouted at me. I think he shouted louder than he would have done had he not been cross with me for wanting the toilet. Anyway it worked in my favour because Mum told *him* off, said I couldn't help it and asked him to stop as soon as he could.

Within five minutes we had stopped in a lay-by with a toilet and – would you believe it? – Dad couldn't wait to go himself.

Back in the car and two mints later, Mum had her tape in again and Rachael and I both started nodding off. We tried to sleep around each other, but my elbow went in her eye and I had a face full of hair. It was about as uncomfortable as trying to sleep in a washing-up bowl full of knives and forks! After ten minutes cramped up, my left leg went to sleep but unfortunately the rest of me stayed awake and so I gave up.

Soon we were driving through the North York Moors. Dad said we would soon see the 'giant golf balls'; they're buildings that look like giant golf balls with radar or something in them, and he always makes a joke about a giant playing golf with them. Unfortunately for Dad they'd been dismantled.

The roads were like a roller coaster – up and down with lots of sharp bends – the only real difference being that round every bend there was a woolly sheep looking at you. One even walked into the middle of the road and stopped. Dad said a rude word and had to brake. Rachael, who loves animals, told him off.

Dad said an even ruder word up the next hill. It was so rude that Mum made him apologize to me and Rachael. The car jerked a bit, coughed and then drove on very slowly, sounding more like a clapped-out lorry than a car.

'The exhaust pipe's gone!' said Dad.

'Where's it gone?' I asked, thinking that a joke might cheer him up.

Dad ignored me. The car wheezed into the side of the road.

'The car needs to use your inhaler!' I said, trying one last joke. My dad has asthma.

'Shut up, Robert!' said Dad. Some people just don't have a sense of humour.

Dad put on the hazard warning lights and disappeared under the car. After a minute he said that word again and came out doing a dance. 'I've burnt my hand!' he said.

Mum got out, looked at it and said it served him right, he should have known it would be hot, and it was no reason to use bad language in front of the children. Dad said that next time he cut his leg off he would say, 'Oh dear me, I've just cut my leg off!' and Mum got back in the car looking very cross.

Rachael and I kept quiet.

Dad disappeared again. After a few minutes he informed us that the exhaust pipe had a hole in it. He went to the boot, took out a round tin and dived back under the car. When he re-surfaced, his hands were black, his hair had exploded and his face was smudged.

'You've got more of that stuff on you than on the exhaust pipe!' said Mum in that voice that she uses to remind us that she does the washing.

'I think that will hold it!' Dad replied.

'I hope so,' said Mum. 'We haven't budgeted for a new exhaust pipe.'

Dad explained how he had put some paste around the hole which would set hard.

'Does that mean your face and hands will set hard and you will turn into a statue?' I asked, but Dad ignored me. He let the engine run for a minute. We all sucked a mint, except me – I crunched mine again. Dad checked under the car and we set off.

We drove so slowly I thought we would be overtaken by one of the sheep. Two cars hooted their horns at us, which made Dad mad. Eventually he seemed to think the paste was set and we went back to a decent speed – for a bike with a puncture – and so we drove on, up and down the hills that lead to Whitby.

3. Welcome to Whitby

We arrived at our holiday cottage at about two o'clock. Cook Street. We all piled out. Dad got down on his knees and I wondered if he was thanking God for the repair holding, but he was just checking the paste. 'I've done a good job there,' he boasted, which I translated from Dadspeak as, 'I got away with that; I wonder how long it will be before it drops to bits!'

My dad is useless at Do It Yourself. He once put up a shelf in my room which would have made the Leaning Tower of Pisa look upright, and one night it fell down with all my books on it. Silly me for putting them on the shelf! Mum and Dad came rushing in and Mum went mad. She said the shelf could have landed on my head! Even I didn't believe that! It was on the other side of the bedroom. She also said that the screw holes Dad had drilled looked like the opening to the Channel tunnel. That was true.

'They have to be big enough for the wall plugs!' said Dad.

'But they look as though you were cutting a hole for a new window!' said Mum, who started laughing at her own joke and went back to bed.

Dad told me he'd mend the shelf the next day, and two weeks later he did. I used it for keeping my plastic dinosaur skeleton on. It was the lightest thing I owned.

We were greeted at the door of our cottage by a woman who looked as though she had a pair of tights over her head. Her hair was scraped back and her mouth and eyes were screwed up. In fact she looked as though she was chewing a wasp because her lips kept moving about even when she wasn't talking.

'Mr and Mrs String?'

It was at times like this that Rachael and I became invisible – some adults never seem to notice that we exist, or don't want to.

'Welcome to Whitby. I am Miss Cake, C-A-K-E,' she spelled.

Cake?! I nearly burst trying not to laugh. I tried biting the inside of my mouth. I tried to think of really sad things. But it was no use. I knew I was going to laugh. I resorted to that old trick. As my laugh burst out, I pretended to have a fit of coughing.

Miss Cake gave me the evil eye. 'I am the landlady to all this terrace of cottages. I live in the end one, number one!' She wiped her hands on her apron for no apparent reason. 'Your cottage has been cleaned thoroughly from top to bottom.' She looked at me as though daring me to laugh at the word 'bottom'. I coughed again.

'If you need anything, at any *reasonable* time, you may knock on my cottage door. I have here a list of all the cutlery, china and so on in your cottage. Please sign it when you have checked it, though I assure you that I have made a thorough check down to the last teaspoon. You will then need to bring the list with your deposit of forty pounds to cover any breakages or losses. As I like to say, "Lovely to look at, lovely to use, But broken or lost your deposit you lose!"'

Miss Cake gave a dry sniff. Dad gave Mum one of his looks that meant 'What have we done?' Rachael looked at her feet. I gave a sarcastic sniff of my own. Mum gave me her laser-beam-from-space look. 'Perhaps Robert and Rachael could play in the garden while you show us around . . .' Mum said diplomatically, using the posh voice she uses to impress people or when she's nervous.

Miss Cake gave a sniff which was even bigger than mine. It was like a hoover on full blast! She did not bother to reply to Mum, but turned to go back into the cottage. Mum and Dad swopped smiles and followed her in, Dad pretending to shoot himself in the head with two fingers.

Rachael and I found our way into the back garden. There was a side gate which, apart from the cottages' back doors, was the only way round the back. It was a shared garden – no fences or hedges to divide it up for the individual cottages. It wasn't exactly an adventure playground – just a patch of moth-eaten grass. It looked exactly like our own back garden, though there was a flower bed at the back of Miss Cake's place.

Rachael did three cartwheels. 'Do you like it here, Rob?'

'No,' I said, 'I think it was a "Miss Cake" to come here!'

Rachael did her fake 'Ha Ha!' and went into another gym routine.

Meanwhile I kicked the grass and thought about how brilliant the holiday had been so far! And as for Miss Cake – I didn't like the look of her. She looked like trouble, and I had a feeling our paths were going to cross before this holiday was over.

4. The Great Escape

Later that afternoon I was in trouble again.
We'd had lunch before we left home, but my
body had forgotten and I was thirsty. The
trouble was Mum had forgotten to pack the tea
bags and, as it was Sunday, the village shop was
shut. Mum's mistake was to go and ask Miss
Cake if she could borrow some tea. Miss Cake
said she didn't drink tea – it turned the inside
of your stomach into a tea bag or something –
she only drank cocoa. She made all four of us a
cup of cocoa and brought it round to our
cottage on a tray! I couldn't believe it. I hate
cocoa! Worse, it was in horrible cups with a

picture of a daft-looking doll knitting a scarf. I ask you! Creepy Rachael said it would help her keep fit and went off to get Dad, who was underneath the car again.

I asked Miss Cake if I could have a piece of cake. She didn't think that was funny. She left.

I told Mum I didn't want the cocoa, but she said it was good for me. I said it would only be good for me if it was thrown away, but she said I was being cheeky. I think she was scared in case Miss Cake saw us tip it down the sink. It would probably melt the sink anyway.

I hate cocoa, a) because it gets skin on the top, b) because you always get a slimy, silvery, stringy thing in your mouth when you drink it, and c) because there's always a load of mud in the bottom of the cup. It's not quite as bad with hot chocolate. I think cocoa must be African for 'mud'.

Anyway, I said I didn't want it. Mum said Miss Cake had made it specially, and it was very kind of her; I said she needn't have bothered. Dad came in from looking at the exhaust pipe.

Now, when something goes wrong with the car Dad's either in a bad mood or will do anything for a quiet life. Just my luck, that afternoon he wanted a quiet life *and* was in a bad mood. And he took Mum's side. He said I *had* to drink the cocoa. I said it was cruel to make children drink mud and I was going to ring Childline. Dad said that if I carried on any more he would have to ring Dadline. He said that a child in India would love a cup of cocoa. I said, 'Give me his name and address and I'll send it to him!' Dad said that joke was 'in poor taste'. I said the cocoa was 'in poor taste' and I was sent to bed. Mum's last words were, 'This cocoa will still be here in the morning!'

There was only one thing for it: it was the cocoa or me. If they chose to keep a cup of cocoa rather than their only son, the son had to go.

I decided to run away – something I decide to do every other week. I once even got to the end of our road with a suitcase, but then I got homesick and came back.

I was sitting on my bed. Downstairs I could hear muffled voices. I couldn't make out what Mum and Dad were saying but it would be things like: 'Where did we go wrong?' . . . 'We don't have this trouble with his sister' . . . 'When I was a boy my best ever treat was a cup of cocoa' . . . 'If we sell the car maybe we could afford to send him to boarding school' . . . I knew I had to escape.

I didn't dare creep downstairs. Mum can hear me from about ten miles away. The only chance was out of the window. I could knot my sheets together to make a rope. Curses! Thank you, Miss Cake, the bed had a duvet. I'd only got one sheet. If I tied one end to my bed I'd just about reach halfway across the carpet. So much for my escape.

I decided to try Plan B. I took a handkerchief out of my suitcase. It had my initial 'R' in the corner – a present from Aunty Beryl – just in case I forgot what my name is, I suppose. I never used it anyway – I use tissues or my sleeve! But now this hanky could be useful. I would use humour, my secret weapon.

Mum and Dad were watching TV while Rachael was practising cartwheels behind the settee. If *I* did that I'd be shot, but never mind that now. I stood in the doorway waving my hanky like a white flag of surrender. No-one noticed. I waved really hard. Still no-one noticed. I coughed. I coughed again.

'Have you got a cough?' asked Mum.

'At least he's using his handkerchief,' said Dad.

I gave up and decided to go out. No-one stopped me or said a word.

5. Football and a Friend

I should remind you that the gardens of the holiday cottages were really just one long strip of grass. About three doors down a boy of about my age was kicking a football. He was trying a few tricks and, as always, I thought I could do better even if I couldn't. Maybe we could play football together and he could be Barnet. Dad was always saying he would play football with me, but at the last minute he always had an asthma attack or found something really important to do like reading the paper.

I ambled over. 'Hi,' I said.

The boy ignored me and kept fooling around with the ball.

'Hello,' I said again. Still no response. This boy was, a) stupid, b) deaf, c) a foreigner. Just my luck.

'Fancy a game?' I asked in my last desperate attempt at communication.

'All right, providing I'm not Manchester United!'

The 'boy' had turned round and it *wasn't* a boy. It was a girl. Short hair, jeans. Perhaps I needed my eyes testing.

And now, what was I to do? Could I, Robert String, ever be seen playing football with a *girl*? It was unheard of. Bogger Pitman would tease me to death and back again if he ever knew. But then again, here I was at Whitby, miles away from Bogger and everyone else at school. The choice was clear: football or return to the land of cocoa.

'Right!' I said. 'I'll be Manchester United. You can be Barnet.'

'Barnet?' said the girl. 'Can't I be a football team?'

'Barnet *are* a football team. Well, sort of. They're my dad's favourite team. Oh, my name's Rob.'

'Hello. I'm Lisa.'

The formalities over, we got down to important business. We made two goals with some sticks and started playing. This was going to be easy. Manchester United versus Barnet! Boy versus girl! Easy peasy lemon squeezy.

After about fifteen minutes the score was 10–3. Unfortunately this was the only time in history that Barnet was to beat Manchester United. I began to think of David and Goliath.

Lisa was good or I was useless. Probably a bit of both.

Now I don't know if I am a bad loser or if I was jealous or what, but I was getting increasingly fed up. Every time I got the ball, Lisa did an ace tackle and I lost it. Eventually I'd had enough and when it was my turn for yet another centre kick, I gave the ball the biggest wellie in history. It was so powerful that it could have punctured the ball. Instead, the ball shot off at about a million miles an hour. Lisa threw herself out of its path and it landed with a big *thwack!* in Miss Cake's flower bed right at the end of the garden.

Even as we ran to collect the ball, we could see the damage. It looked as if a hurricane had hit it. About ten flowers had been decapitated and were lying flat in a pool of pink and red petals.

And, of course, because it was me who had kicked the ball, the flowers *had* to belong to Miss Cake, and she *had* to be looking through her window at the time.

We were standing right in the middle of the wreckage when she came out, her hoover nose working overtime. We were vandals, a disgrace to our parents, wreckers of the environment – we were probably personally responsible for destroying the ozone layer. As she droned on, she picked up bits of flowers as if she was collecting up a bouquet, then suddenly, more like a four-year-old than an adult, she seemed to go completely bonkers and threw the whole lot up in the air to rain over us like confetti at a wedding.

Lisa and I were stunned into silence.

Miss Cake stiffened, sniffed a threat to report us to the police, our parents, our school . . . and flounced back in.

'We have just suffered a cake attack!' said Lisa. 'Crumbs!'

We picked up the ball and kicked it around for a while at the 'safe' end of the garden, but it wasn't the same. We gave up and went back into my cottage.

Mum and Dad were sitting at the kitchen table with a jolly-looking woman with glasses. They were all drinking cups of tea – there wasn't a cup of cocoa in sight.

It turned out that this lady was Lisa's mum, Mrs Peak. There was no mention of her dad – it was just the two of them on holiday together.

There was a lot of grown-up conversation that I won't bother you with, except to say that Lisa's mum had brought the tea bags over after she and Mum and Dad had suffered a visit from Miss Cake.

She had jumped up and down and shouted a bit and let off steam about her flowers and, according to Lisa's mum, there then followed a bit of an argument. Not between Miss Cake and our parents, but between Mum and Dad after she'd gone. Dad called Miss Cake 'that loony woman', which Mum said was typical of a man whose idea of gardening was to water the flowers at home with weed killer. Dad said it cut down on the work and Miss Cake should follow his example. It was stupid to put a flower bed on a football pitch anyway!

Instead of Mum shouting at me, she shouted at Dad; and instead of Lisa and me having to apologize, Dad was sent round to Miss Cake to apologize for his rudeness. Brilliant!

String's first rule of survival: blame someone else.

Better still, Miss Cake then apologized to Dad for over-reacting. As Dad said, 'Her bark was worse than her bite.' He ended up staying for a chat over a cup of cocoa!

It seemed that Lisa and her mum would be in Whitby all the time we were there. They had arrived earlier in the day.

Lisa's mum and my mum and dad got on really well. It was as if she and Mum had been friends for years, and she even seemed to like Dad's boring stories. They spent that evening drinking wine. Rachael showed everyone her handstand into backward roll on the living-room carpet, then went upstairs to read. Lisa and I watched TV.

I can't pretend I was glad she was a girl, but none of my friends from school could see me and she was a laugh. We spent some time trying to guess Miss Cake's first name. Lisa suggested Cherry Cake. I thought of Ginger. In the end Lisa's best idea was Nutty Fruit Cake.

We also tried to make the world's longest rhyme about her. Things like: 'Miss *Cake* was *awake* in a *lake* with Francis *Drake*. Along came a *snake* whose name was *Jake* who looked like a *fake*. She hit him with a *rake* which made him *ache* then *baked* him in a *cake* and that *maked* the earth *quake* and Miss *Cake shake*.' It was all a load of rubbish, but we killed ourselves laughing.

It was thanks to Lisa that Miss Cake's flower bed had exploded – that was bad; but she had got me out of drinking cocoa – that was good. She had all the makings of a good friend for the holiday.

What I didn't know was that Lisa was one of those people who attract trouble like a magnet. Thanks to her I would be stuck in the middle of one heap of trouble after another. You know some people have lucky charms. They nail a horse shoe to the door (once the horse has taken it off). Or they have a rabbit's foot. If I had a rabbit's foot I'd go to the doctor's. No, you know what I mean! They have a rabbit's foot on the end of a key ring or something. It's supposed to be lucky. (Not for the rabbit with only three legs!) Well, Lisa was my charm – my *un*lucky charm. There were times when I wanted to nail her to a door or stick her on the end of a key ring. Life was never boring with her, but boy, did she bring trouble.

And the holiday had only just begun.

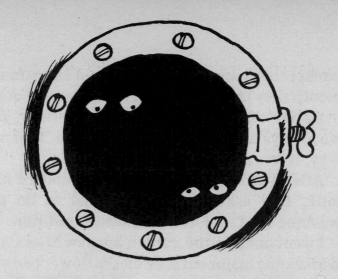

6. The Lifeboat

The next day at breakfast Rachael and I had our traditional argument over who was going to have the free plastic Dog on a Log inside the Chocky Crocky Flakes. I won because Dad said, 'Eldest first', and Rachael could have the next one. I don't know why I bothered: a) I didn't know what I'd do with a Dog on a Log anyway, b) it was a load of rubbish – they ought to pay you to take them away, c) it didn't even look like a Dog on a Log – it looked like a lump of squashed-up red plastic. Never mind: I'd won! When I tasted my Chocky Crocky Flakes I think I'd rather have eaten the Dog on the Log. On the packet they looked chocolatey and crisp. In my mouth they tasted like soggy cardboard. I don't even like cereal! But this was our holiday, and we always had cereal on holiday. Don't ask me why; it was a String family tradition.

After I'd finished eating my cardboard and milk, Dad asked me if I wanted to do the washing up. I said 'No!' – another tradition.

I went out into the garden but saw Miss Cake performing major surgery on the flower bed and dashed back in again. I turned on the TV. There was a singing Dog on a Log advertising Chocky Crocky Flakes. I couldn't believe it. I decided to change the words of the song:

'*Start your day*
The Chocky Crocky way,
They taste like cardboard and they look like
 poo,
Anyone with taste would rather eat a shoe!'

'Robert, please!' It was Mum. 'We have visitors.'

I went into the kitchen. It was Lisa and her mum. Arrangements were being made. Mum and Mrs Peak and Rachael were going shopping. Dad, Lisa and I were going to check out the cost of hiring a boat on the river Esk near

Sleights. If it was cheap enough, our two families were going for a picnic by the river.

By ten o'clock the three of us were on our way. Dad, of course, decided on a detour through Whitby. In fact, if it hadn't been for that, none of this story would have happened, because just by the pier, turning up that steep hill called the Khyber Pass, the exhaust pipe finally went. There was a horrible sound from the car, followed by another horrible sound from Dad.

He pulled into the side of the road. 'Wait here, you two, and don't move!'

I immediately pretended to be a statue, but as no-one noticed I started moving again.

Dad went under the car and came up looking as though he'd lost £100 – which I suppose in a way he had. 'Oh, well, that's another million pounds down the drain! We need a new exhaust pipe! The old one's dropped off!'

'I've told you a hundred thousand times not to exaggerate!' I told him.

Dad sat in the driver's seat and turned the key. It sounded like a tank. The engine was loud and it seemed to be firing its gun. The engine kept making exploding sounds. Dad turned it off. 'There's a garage at the top of this hill. You kids wait here. I'll see if they'll tow me in. I don't think the car will make it up this hill, and – just my luck – it's a one-way street so I can't go back!'

'Can't we come with you?' I asked.

'No, you'll slow me down.'

'You don't have to carry us, Dad. We can walk!'

'Shut up, Robert.'

'Well, can't we explore? It's boring sitting in the car.'

'I tell you what,' said Dad. 'Here's two quid. Go back round the corner: there's an amusement arcade. There's the Lifeboat Museum as well – that's free! I'll meet you there when I've sorted out the car. There are toilets opposite if you need them.' I wondered why they had a lifeboat near the toilets. Perhaps it was in case a sailor got stuck in the loo!

Lisa and I jumped out, leaving Dad to lock up, and dashed down to the arcade. We got our money changed and blew it all in about fifteen seconds. I was going to show off in front of Lisa on that machine where you bash crocodiles with a big hammer, but I only scored eleven – my worst score ever! She scored twenty-three!!

Then I tried to win one of those teddy bears you hook up with a crane. I don't know why, but even if the person before me wins 433 teddy bears, as soon as it is my turn the crane breaks. My aim was perfect. The crane grabbed the teddy bear by one leg and lifted it up in the air. Lisa was dancing with excitement. But, of course, just before the teddy bear came down the trap door, and without me touching a thing, the crane opened up and dropped it. I couldn't believe it – except that it always happens to me.

I'd better not be a real crane driver when I leave school. Can you imagine? I'd be carrying a big heavy girder with my crane and I'd drop it. Right on top of a Rolls-Royce!

Lisa went off to complain but I told her I wasn't bothered. £2 down the pan!

We wandered into the Lifeboat Museum, our heads down as we walked past the charity boxes in the shape of lifeboats. We looked at the bookmarks and pencils and things, then went into the museum proper. There were lots of old photos of men with big hats and big beards, all looking like Captain Bird's-Eye. There were models in glass cases, including one which looked as though my dad had made it. I think it was supposed to be a boat after it had been wrecked in a storm!

Round the corner, best of all, was Whitby's

old lifeboat – the real thing. You went up some steps that took you to a platform alongside so you could see inside. Lisa wanted to get in which wasn't allowed. But there was no-one about. It would be easy. We looked around, jumped over the barrier, and down onto the boat. One last check to make sure no-one could see us, then we opened the cabin door and went in.

It was quite small and very spooky – plus I was scared of getting caught. I was just hanging about really, wanting to get out as quickly as possible, but Lisa was messing about saying 'Aye aye, cap'n' and 'Land ahoy!' and so on, while opening all the cupboards.

Then I grabbed her arm. 'Lisa, shhh!'

Someone was coming. I could hear voices, men's voices. They were on the platform by the side of the boat, less than a metre from where we were.

The men had stopped there and they were talking. They obviously couldn't see us, hidden in the cabin, and so they didn't think that anyone could hear them.

What they had to say would make the hair on a completely bald person's head stand up on end.

7. The Plot Thickens

They couldn't see us and we couldn't see them, but we could hear snatches of what they were saying. It was all a bit muffled, like listening to voices in another room, or as if they were talking with their mouths full of socks.

At first I was bothered that they would catch us hiding and report us, but then I started trying to hear what they were saying.

'Are you sure it's safe here?' asked a voice that sounded as thick as a bag of potatoes.

'Yes. Stop worrying. This is perfect. If anyone sees us, they'll think we're just looking at the lifeboat.'

'Well, we are looking at the lifeboat.'

'Yes, I know that.' The second voice also sounded thick, but not quite as thick. 'But we're really here to finish our plans. If anyone sees us then we *pretend* that we are looking at the lifeboat.'

'But I'm not pretending. I really am looking at the lifeboat.'

'Yes, I know,' said the other, obviously losing patience, 'but that's just an excuse. We're really here to plan the robbery!'

Well, when he said 'robbery' I nearly fell over-board. I grabbed Lisa's arm. I wanted to speak but she gave me a look and I kept quiet.

The man continued, 'This is our last chance to check everything until we meet at the bank tomorrow night at midnight.'

'At midnight?'

'That's when the big and little hands are on the twelve and when it's dark. We meet outside the bank. I'll park the car on New Quay Road.'

'New Quay Road?'

'Yes, that's where the bank is. So when we've finished the robbery we can drive away. We can't carry all that money in carrier bags! We need a car.'

'And you are sure we can get in?'

'What – into the car?'

'No, the bank!'

'Of course we can get in. You can't rob a bank unless you can get in. Give me strength!'

'What about the vault?' said the thick one.

'It's a big safe where they keep all the money.'

'I know that – how do we get in it?'

'Through the door. Don't worry about it. All you have to do is carry the money. You're there to use your muscles, not your brain. That's *my* job.'

I leaned forward. I was going to risk looking through one of the portholes. I wanted to see these men.

It was a waste of time. All I could see was the barrier that Lisa and I had jumped over. One of the men was holding the barrier as he spoke and I could see his hand. Brilliant. I'd have to tell the police I'd seen a hand planning a bank robbery. What could I tell them? It had four fingers and a thumb and was covered in skin. Knowing my luck it would be in disguise.

But then I did notice something. The thumbnail was that blacky, purply, yellow colour you get when you try to bang in a nail with a hammer, and miss, and hit your thumb instead – like Dad does when he Does it Himself. A

43

clue! Sherlock String was on the case.

'Now – any questions?'

'When do I get my share?' asked Mr Potato.

'You won't get anything unless you're there at midnight.'

The strange thing was that the voices didn't seem to fit in with where the hand was. They seemed to be coming from my left. The hand was on my right. Perhaps one of them had a really long arm. Perhaps he was a giant. Perhaps there was someone else there as well; someone who had not spoken. It was impossible to tell. Looking through the porthole wasn't easy either. It was like looking through the bottom of a jam jar – with jam still in it!

I could hear footsteps walking away in opposite directions, and down the two sets of steps. Suddenly there was a big crash. One of the men had fallen. 'Ooh, my head!' It was Mr Potato. The idiot had fallen down the stairs. He picked himself up noisily and left the museum.

Lisa stood up. I held back for a moment. We didn't want to be seen now.

After a minute that seemed like an eternity, we ventured out of the cabin, looked briefly around, and climbed over the side of the boat back onto the platform. There was no-one about.

'What are we going to do?' asked Lisa.

'We must find Dad and tell him.'

'Tell him what?'

'The truth. We heard some men planning to rob the National Midway Bank tomorrow night!'

'How do you know it's the National Midway?'

'Because that's the bank on New Quay Road – we passed it today. It's my mum and dad's bank; they're always using the cash machine.'

'Come on then,' said Lisa, 'let's find your dad. But I know what will happen! He won't believe a word of it!'

8. Our Story

Mum, Mrs Peak and Rachael were all waiting with Dad by the car. Mrs Peak's car had its hazard lights on. They had finished their shopping and had been waiting back at our cottage. Dad had phoned them from the garage.

'Where have you two been?' snapped Dad. He was in a bad mood because of the car – Mum would have blamed him for the exhaust pipe.

'Dad! Dad!' and I blurted it all out in a big rush.

As soon as I had said it out loud I knew that Lisa had been right. It sounded like a load of rubbish.

'Robin Banks, eh?' He gave Lisa's mum a sideways look. 'Is he a friend of Jim Nastics and Ivor Bignose?'

Lisa scowled. 'No, honestly, Mr String – it's true. Mum . . . Mrs String . . .' She looked from one to the other in despair, begging to be believed.

Dad looked a bit crumpled. Mind you, he always did that when no-one laughed at his jokes. 'Robert.' He called me that when he was serious. 'You mustn't be silly. It was just some people messing about!'

I was actually beginning to doubt it myself. Maybe they were just people being stupid, but before I could say anything Mum started off full blast.

'Look, you two – if this is some sort of joke, I'm not in the mood. The exhaust pipe's gone on the car and that means I'm in a bad mood anyway . . .' She paused to see if we would back down. 'If you are serious, then we go *straight* round to the police.'

This was my chance. I was just about to say to forget it when—

'To the police it is,' said Lisa. 'But I know what will happen. They won't believe a word of it.'

9. Down at the Station

A big, burly sergeant was standing behind the desk in the police station. He was writing something in a big book when we went in and didn't even look up. We waited for a minute or two, then Mum, who was getting really het up, interrupted him.

'Excuse me, officer, but these children have a crime to report!'

'A crime? Well, you've come to the right place. This is a police station.' He gave a funny little laugh. He made a big deal about putting a full stop at the end of his writing and looked me straight in the eye. 'What sort of

48

crime? Someone kidnapped your hamster?'

'A bank robbery!' Lisa jumped in.

'A bank robbery.' The sergeant picked up his pencil and sucked at the end. 'Someone's robbed your piggy bank?'

Lisa wiped the smile off his face. I almost believed her myself. She told him all about the lifeboat and the voices and the time and the place and the name of the bank, and I told him about the thumbnail and how the man had fallen down the stairs.

'And you say these men sounded – not very bright?'

'Thick!' I said.

'But you didn't see them. Mmmm.' He said nothing more. He stood up and went into a back office. We could see the shape of his body through the frosted glass. He was talking to another policeman. Then he picked up a telephone and spoke for a minute or two. When he returned, he was wearing a helmet.

He took our names and addresses: my mum and dad's names, Lisa's mum's name. It was then I learnt that her parents were divorced. He also took our holiday addresses. He wrote it all down – very slowly.

'Right, you lot. I don't believe a word of it. If

you heard anything, I think you heard some people messing about.' He gave us a look that meant we had one more chance to confess that we had made it all up. I was too scared to speak. 'But we can't take any chances. We're off to the bank. The manager happens to be a friend of mine,' and he wheeled us through the door.

Dad and Rachael were going back to the cottages with Lisa's mum and would meet us there. Mum, Lisa and I went with the sergeant. We were off to the National Midway Bank.

10. Mr Seymour

The bank was on the corner of the road opposite the swing bridge. We walked there.

We were met at the door by a young lady in a grey uniform. She didn't wait for us to speak. 'Mr Seymour is expecting you. Please come in.'

We were taken to a dark wooden door with a spy hole in it and a name plate saying: MR I SEYMOUR, MANAGER. I was going to make a joke about 'I See More' and the spy hole – but there's a time and a place for everything, as Dad would say.

'Mr Seymour,' said the lady and showed us in.

Mr Seymour was a big smiling man with a

sweaty, balding head and a rather crumpled grey suit. 'Sergeant Jenkins – Ray, come in, come in. And this must be Robert and Lisa . . . and Robert's mum, is it? Mrs String? Janet, some tea, please. And some orange for the young detectives.'

'And some biscuits, sir?'

'Yes, please,' and he winked at me. I hate it when grown-ups wink at me; it always looks as if they've got something in their eye, but in the circumstances I smiled.

Mr Seymour sat behind his desk, his hands in his jacket pockets, smiling broadly. 'Now, Robert, Lisa. The sergeant here has told me all about your story. Will you tell it to me?'

We looked at one another, then, taking it in turns, for the third time that day we told our story. We told him about the lifeboat and the two men, one thick, one even thicker, and the hand with my one clue – the black nail. 'If he won't own up we could *blacknail* him!' I said. The sergeant and Mum gave me dirty looks. I was caught in their cross fire.

Mr Seymour smiled, but that was because he was smiling all the time. He reminded me of the vicar who comes into school to do assemblies every now and then. He has a permanent smile on his face. It doesn't matter what happens. Once he was telling a story and a kid in the front row was sick on his shoes. He still kept smiling. Well, Mr Seymour was just the same.

Janet came in with the drinks and biscuits. The sergeant tucked in.

'Well,' said Mr Seymour, 'it certainly sounds like this bank. The point is, if Robert and Lisa are right in what they say, do we take it seriously? What do you think, Sergeant?'

'I don't know, sir.' The sergeant shook his head. 'I suppose I could spare a constable to guard the bank, but' – he looked at me and Lisa – 'it will be a *very very* expensive mistake if you two are making this up. And if you are . . . for heaven's sake tell us now, before it's too late.'

We said nothing.

'Mrs String?'

Poor Mum. You could see her torn between loyalty to me and her own doubts. 'Sergeant, Mr Seymour: Robert can be naughty, he can be silly' – Thanks a bunch, Mum, I thought – 'but he is *not* a liar. He may have been mistaken in what he heard but he is not making it up. I think they are telling the truth.'

It was like a weight off my back. I sighed with

relief and smiled at Mum and at Lisa. The policeman and Mr Seymour stood up.

We were told that the arrangements would all be dealt with, which was a polite way of telling us to get lost. We did this happily.

'Whatever happens, Mrs String, I will be back to see you.' Those were the sergeant's last words as we left.

11. The Night of the Robbery

Lisa and I were kept very busy for the rest of that day and the next – our parents saw to that – but all we could think about was the robbery. Whitby had clouded over in any case, so we spent most of our time indoors. We played about 350 games of Snap. I won two!

The next night, Tuesday, was the night of the robbery. Lisa and I persuaded Dad to drive us past the bank four times. We were too excited to sleep and our mums said we could stay up. We said Dad could test his new exhaust pipe. We were out until twelve thirty. We saw – nothing: no car – not even a bike – parked outside. No men in black-and-white jerseys and masks, carrying bags reading SWAG. We couldn't even see a policeman – but perhaps he was hiding inside or was disguised as a lamp post or something. And there was nothing on the news either; we watched especially.

We expected a visit from the police the next day, but it was not until Thursday afternoon that Mum had a telephone call asking us to go round to the police station.

Soon Lisa and I plus Mum and Lisa's mum were sitting in a small room. Dad was left at the cottage to look after you-know-who. Mr Seymour was there too, still sweating and still smiling. Somehow it made the sergeant's cross face look even crosser.

'Well, you two,' said Sergeant Jenkins. 'Mr Seymour and I have been put to a *lot* of trouble. Both Tuesday and Wednesday night I had a police officer inside the bank. Mr Seymour had a member of his staff there as well – Mr Possett.

'Nothing – I repeat, *nothing* – happened. No-one came into the bank, no-one broke in, no-one even knocked on the door and ran away.' He paused to check that we were both looking suitably guilty, and that our two mums looked embarrassed. 'In fact,' he continued, 'according to my constable, the most interesting thing that he did was to listen to Mr Possett snoring.'

He leaned closer to us. 'Well?'

I wanted to say, 'Yes, very well, thank you,' but I knew that wasn't what he meant. We kept our heads down.

'Nothing to say, eh?' The sergeant sighed. 'You know that wasting police time is a serious offence, do you? The police are too busy to go wasting their nights sitting inside a bank twiddling their thumbs.'

He looked across at Mr Seymour, who didn't seem at all bothered. He was still smiling and still had his hands in his pockets. If I ever have my hands in my pockets I get shouted at. Just because he was a bank manager! It wasn't fair. Typical of grown-ups. I remember one teacher at school shouting at us to stay on the path and keep off the grass – and all the time he was standing on the grass himself!

'It will be up to Mr Seymour here to say if he wants to press charges.'

I thought he ought to press his suit first, but I just looked up at Mr Seymour with that little lost puppy look that always works with Mum.

'Sergeant' – he smiled – 'I have a suggestion.' He looked at Lisa and me. 'I think these two young people should come to the bank with me and apologize to Mr Possett. Other than that' – he smiled even more broadly – 'well, we were all young once. I'm sure Robert and Lisa did not mean to cause so much trouble. They just heard some people messing about, or perhaps they misheard. I say: forgive and forget.'

My mum stood up. I thought she was going to give Mr Seymour a kiss. A truly revolting thought! She didn't. 'Oh, Mr Seymour, that is *so* kind of you – isn't it, Robert? What do you say?'

Neither of us really felt like saying anything. It was good not to be in trouble, but we knew what we had heard. I mumbled a thank-you.

Anyway, what happened was that Lisa and I went with Mr Seymour to the bank while the two mums stayed behind to fill in some papers and to be told off, in a grown-up sort of way, for letting me and Lisa be stupid or for wasting police time.

As we were going Mum said, 'Robert, we'll meet you at the bank in about twenty minutes. Don't wander off – and say thank you!'

If I'd only known what was going to happen, I'd have broken the habit of a lifetime and given

Mum a hug and a kiss goodbye. It was going to be a *lot* longer than twenty minutes before I'd see her again – and at times I thought I'd never see her again.

Mr. Eric Possett

12. Mr Possett

It was really dark and cloudy as we walked to the bank and I felt a few spots of rain and wished I'd put on my coat. Lisa and I were both wearing jeans and T-shirts.

Mr Seymour didn't speak to us as we walked. He just kept his hands in his pockets and smiled and nodded at one or two people – probably customers at the bank.

When we arrived, Lisa opened the door for him, which was a bit creepy of her, but then he called Janet over and told her to go and get us both an ice cream and I felt a bit rotten. He told us he had a few phone calls to make and went into his office while we sat on grey chairs.

Janet bought us each a '99' ice cream and whispered, 'Don't worry, kids. Mr Seymour is OK. He likes you – I can tell.'

I was just about to take my first lick when a man, one of the bank staff, called us over. As soon as I saw him, I knew I didn't like him. He was sitting behind a glass partition at the counter. He had a name plate: MR ERIC POSSETT. He wore a jacket that was too small for him even though he was as thin as a skeleton on a diet. His skin was tight and shiny and his eyes were small and half-open in their hollow sockets. His nose would have looked all right on a baby. On a man, it looked as though it hadn't been properly finished.

'So you are the children who ruined my beauty sleep,' he said. He looked as though he'd had plenty of ugly sleep instead. 'Do you realize I've had to spend two nights here, locked in with an idiot policeman, waiting for non-existent men to stage a non-existent robbery?'

'We're sorry!' said Lisa.

I felt ice cream dripping onto my hand, but didn't dare lick it off.

'Sorry?' he spluttered. '*Sorry?* What about my wasted time? All because of some ridiculous children's game!' He was stooped forward and hunched like a vulture. He looked as though he was sitting on the toilet.

A blob of ice cream fell onto his counter. Just my luck! Mr Possett leaned even further forward, glaring. He opened his mouth and looked as though he was going to shout. I waited to have my brain blown out, but he was cut off by Janet.

'This way,' she called. We left Mr Possett with his mouth open and went towards the office. I dared one final look back. He stared at me with his beady eyes, turned away and reached for his telephone. I went through the door.

Mr Seymour was leaning back in his chair. 'Come in, Lisa, come in, Robert. Come and sit down.'

We both did as we were told. I didn't really know what to do with my ice cream. Was it ruder to eat it while he was talking to us, or ruder to leave it to melt? We both started licking.

'Now, children, first of all don't worry about Mr Possett. I will see to him. He's not really our kind of person, I'm afraid. He was sent here by head office – I didn't appoint him myself. According to the police, he spent most of his time guarding the bank fast asleep anyway.'

I felt myself beginning to relax.

'Nevertheless, Lisa and Robert, you did cause us some problems.'

I stiffened again.

'You see, you made a lot of trouble for the police and for us here at the bank. We all had to give up a lot of time, and time is money – I should know: I run a bank.' He sniggered at his own joke. 'I need to be sure, absolutely sure, that once you leave here, we won't hear any more about it.'

I wanted to say, 'Yes, OK. I'm sorry – I must have had a brainstorm or something,' but Lisa couldn't keep her mouth shut.

'But we know what we heard. If it had just been one of us, you could say it was a dream or a hallucination or a mirage – but not both of us. We know what we heard. And OK, something stopped the robbery – maybe the robbers saw the policeman or something, maybe they chickened out – I don't know; but I do know what I heard. Maybe we've saved the bank millions of pounds. We haven't made anything up!'

'And Robert?' Mr Seymour smiled at me. He must have seen that I looked less certain.

'I'm sorry,' I said. 'We didn't mean to waste your time. Perhaps it was people messing about.

But perhaps something went wrong. One of them was so thick he probably robbed himself by mistake.'

'We're not going to give up,' said Lisa. 'One way or another, we'll persuade the police.'

Mr Seymour leaned back even further – I thought he was going to fall backwards. Then, as if he had been pushed by an invisible hand, he lurched forward, picked up the telephone on his desk and dialled a number. 'Excuse me.' He smiled at us.

A tiny voice answered the phone. 'The answer is "no",' said Mr Seymour and put the phone down.

'I'm sorry about that,' he said. 'I just remembered I needed to let some clients know that I had turned down their request for a loan. I hate breaking bad news.' He looked up as if he was lost for words and his script was printed on the ceiling.

'Robert and Lisa, you are good children. If I had children of my own, I would want them to be like you – brave and honest. You believed what you heard and did the right thing.' He licked his lips and smiled again. 'I wish there were more people like you' – he sighed – 'and less people like our Mr Possett! Let us forgive

and forget.' He stood up. 'Well, I see you have
finished your ice creams. It's time for you to go
back to your mothers. It has been a pleasure to
know you.'

I thought he was going to shake hands or give
us a certificate or something: it was like being
in an assembly at school.

'Come through this back door – it's quicker
and more private. This way you won't have to
bump into Mr Possett again! My special door. I
asked the sergeant to drop your mothers right
outside.'

We turned to go.

'Robert and Lisa – goodbye.'

We were out in a side street behind the bank.
The street was empty. Perhaps it was the rain.
It was pouring now, and there were black clouds
above. Lovely weather for a summer holiday!

Lisa and I looked round for our mums.

'They must still be at the police station,' said
Lisa. 'Let's go back inside.'

We turned and tried the door, but it was
locked. We heard screeching brakes and a car
skidded to a stop behind us. I guessed it was the
police, but I couldn't have been more wrong.

The driver and passenger got out. Both wore
dark clothes; one was thin and weedy, one fat.

The thin one spoke. 'Robert and Lisa?'

Straight away I knew that these were the men from the lifeboat.

'Is this them?' asked the other one. It was Mr Potato. No doubt about it. He looked as stupid as he sounded. In fact his face looked just like a big spud. But stupid or not, he could hurt us, and when he grabbed for us we ran.

The thin one tried to catch Lisa. She kicked him hard where it hurts. He swore and doubled up.

Mr Potato threw himself at me but I ducked and he fell heavily, right in the middle of a puddle.

'Run for it, Lisa!' I shouted.

We ran – ran for our lives – charging through the streets of Whitby, the two men close at our heels.

13. Hunted

They say an animal being chased by hunters runs wildly, not caring where it goes, not thinking ahead, just trying to escape. That was us. Thinking back, we should have run to the police station or back into the bank. But our brains weren't working properly. With those two men after us, all we wanted to do was get away.

There weren't even any people to run to. It was pouring with rain, coming down in sheets. There were hollow rolls of thunder and flashes of eye-dazzling lightning.

So we ran blindly, soaked and terrified. The

two men cursed us as they charged behind.

'I'll get the car!' shouted the thin man. 'You keep running!'

'But I've got a stitch,' said Mr Potato.

'Well, sew it up. Keep after them.'

We had a chance. If we could just use our brains we were at an advantage. Two children, two brains – against one potato, no brain.

My family had been to Whitby loads of times, so I knew where we were heading. We hared over the swing bridge, left up Sandgate past the museum right into the market place.

Sheltering under the art centre in the market place was a miserable-looking woman with two miserable-looking children. They had matching blue anoraks and all three were dripping wet from the rain. We would have just a few seconds before Mr Potato rolled into sight.

Lisa and I ran up to her. We must have looked a sight. Our T-shirts and jeans were sopping wet, our hair was plastered all over our faces, and we could hardly speak we were so out of breath.

'Help! Help us, please!' I implored. 'There's a man after us!'

'Great!' said one of the kids. 'Can I play?'

'This isn't a game, you stupid idiot – it's for

real!' I shouted, and the little boy started crying. That was a bit of a mistake really.

'Don't you shout at my Norman,' said the woman, shouting at me herself. 'He only wants to play. Go and play your silly games somewhere else.' She paused, bent down and gave Norman a hug. Then she straightened up and I thought that the penny had finally dropped and she would help us. I was wrong! 'And if I was your mother I wouldn't let you play out in this weather. Don't you know it's dangerous to be outside in a thunderstorm?'

'Sorry,' I said. 'Next time I'm about to be murdered I'll make sure it's a sunny day!'

The woman's face looked like a boil about to burst, but before she could do anything we heard a noise that put everything else out of our minds. It was a car. It was coming from the right, up Church Street towards the market place, and it was being driven by the thin man. At the same moment Mr Potato staggered into view looking like my dad having a major asthma attack.

There were three escape routes. Two were blocked; the only way out was left up Church Street and try to beat the car to the steps that led to the church.

What I really wanted to do was grab Norman

and throw him in front of the car – then he'd really be in our game, but instead I grabbed his mum's shopping bag and dumped it in the middle of the road, spilling all her groceries. She screamed and ran after me, picking things up off the soaking wet road and making a very effective barrier.

This gave us a few precious seconds. I shouted to Lisa to follow me and ran as fast as I could up the cobblestones of Church Street. Mr Potato couldn't believe it. For a moment he seemed rooted to the spot – then, as if someone had suddenly switched his motor on, he sprang into life and started running after us.

We ran as fast as we could in the still driving rain. The road came to a dead end. We were faced with the steep, wet, slippery 199 steps that led up to St Mary's Church. We had no choice. Climb.

We went up two or three steps at a time. My lungs were bursting.

If this had been an old film Lisa would have fallen and twisted her ankle and I would have carried her to the top. This was not a film, and a third of the way up it was me who fell. My trainer only half made it to the step and, perhaps because it was so wet, sort of slid sideways and backwards. I went with it. I lay sprawled on the steps.

Lisa stopped, came back and helped me up. We could see Mr Potato at the bottom of the steps, standing by the car, which had come to a stop there. Suddenly it reversed. It was obviously going back the long way round up to the top of the hill to try and cut us off between St Mary's and the ruined abbey. Somehow we had to beat it to the top.

I stood up.

'Are you OK?' Lisa asked.

'Yes!' I lied. My ankle was killing me.

'We've got to keep going!' said Lisa. And she was right: Mr Potato was starting up the 199 steps.

I struggled on. Funnily enough, as we approached the top the pain in my ankle eased. I knew I'd twisted it badly but it wasn't hurting nearly as much.

We threw ourselves up the last few steps. Looking back, we saw Mr Potato about three-quarters of the way up. He didn't look very healthy. In fact he looked as though his lungs had burst! He was wheezing like a completely unfit, fat man trying to run up some very steep steps, which is what he was.

There was a screech of brakes: the car arriving at the car park on the other side of the church. Once again, it was two against two. The only way to go was into the church and, grabbing Lisa, I ran for the door and went in.

14. Sanctuary

St Mary's Church is not like any other church I've ever been in. Not that I've been in that many. Every time we come to Whitby, though, we go round St Mary's Church. It's got no lights and there's this weird three-layered pulpit with its own ear trumpets because in Victorian times one of the vicars had a deaf wife. There's a tiny little museum in one corner with an Anglo-Saxon baby's coffin made of stone. Rachael thinks that's really spooky. And round the walls there are huge boards with inscriptions from the Bible. It's really strange.

But the strangest of all are the pews – the

benches people sit on. They're not open like in other churches. They are all enclosed. They have wooden panels all round them – with a door for you to get in. They're called 'box pews' and they really do look as if they're boxed in. The boxes are really high. Even an adult would have to go right up to them to see in. They would make an excellent hiding place.

We ran past the entrance where they sell bookmarks and cards, and into the main part of the church.

'This way,' I said. We ran in and I threw open one of the doors. We pulled it shut behind us, locked the little brass bolt, and sat on the hard wooden pew, trying to get our breath back. Lisa wiped her face with her T-shirt and I did the same. Our shirts were sopping wet so it didn't dry us, but it was refreshing.

For a few glorious minutes we were out of danger. We just sat and steamed.

Again, if this had been a film we'd have made a plan: turned the pew into a glider and flown out, or dug a tunnel. I saw this programme on telly once where a man was trapped in an old gold mine. His dog happened to be passing and saw what was going on. This dog ran back to town, where he contacted the sheriff, told him the man was injured and which baddies had done it, and gave directions how to get to the mine. All this in woofs. Unfortunately we didn't have a dog! We just sat there. We were both in a state of shock, soaking wet and tired.

Not, of course, for long. We heard Mr Potato blunder into the church. There's a notice when you first come in saying MIND THE STEP. He fell over it.

I peered over the top of the box pew. He was walking slowly down the aisle of the church, looking into every pew. We could hear him every step of the way. Nearer and nearer to us.

'Come on!' I said and I touched Lisa's arm. She followed as I climbed over the panel at the back of the pew into the pew next door.

Mr Potato saw us and shouted out.

And so began a game of cat and mice – or should I say, potato and children. Every time he got near us, we dodged out of one pew into the next. I suppose we could have gone on like this for ever, but then Mr Potato had a crash. If he'd been driving a car he'd have crashed into a tree; as he was in a church he crashed into a vicar!

The vicar was reading some papers. He was obviously as blind as a bat because he held his papers about five centimetres from his face. As he came round the corner he and Mr Potato met head on. The two fell to the floor in a tangle of arms and legs, the vicar underneath. He said something that was not very religious and passed out. We threw open the door of our pew and ran out. Straight into the arms of the thin man.

IN LOVING
MEMORY
OF
The Count

15. The Graveyard

'Got you!' he said.

'No you haven't,' I said, and pushed past him into the graveyard. Lisa was not so lucky.

St Mary's churchyard is a perfect setting for a horror story – in fact the book *Dracula* has some scenes set there. It's full of gravestones that are made of some soft stone – sandstone, I think. Anyway, because the churchyard's at the top of a sixty-metre cliff, and because the weather at Whitby can be wild, these gravestones have been worn into strange, grotesque shapes. They look like rows of jagged, rotten teeth. It's really spooky.

You can imagine what it was like in a thunderstorm: the dark, purple clouds, the flashes of zigzag lightning, the driving wind, the rain pounding at my face and stinging my eyes. And in all this I was running – running like a frightened rabbit from a hunter, weaving in and out of the graves.

I was a kid. I was wet. I was tired. And I was being chased by a giant potato. He'd recovered from his crash with the vicar and was after me.

Most of the grass in the graveyard is long, and in the wet it was slippery. It whipped at my legs, which were red and stinging in my jeans. I kept upright by grabbing the gravestones as I weaved in and out. The stone was rough and worn away, and it cut into my hands, but all I was bothered about was getting away.

Mr Potato was shouting at me. I heard him fall over – he was good at that. He heaved himself up with one thought in his mind: to get me.

I was tiring. Although my bad ankle wasn't hurting it wasn't working properly – it slowed me down. Well, that's my excuse. The truth is, the rain and just being tired out from all that running was getting to me.

I made one last frantic effort. I almost threw

myself for the gateway that led out to the car park.

What happened next was a bit of a blur. I think he jumped at me. It was like a rugby tackle. Anyway, he was lying full length in the mud, his fat hand gripped around my ankle. It was my bad one too. I kicked out with my good leg but he pulled me down to the ground and I skewed round. There was a single gravestone, set apart from the others for some reason, right on the edge of the cliff top. I skidded on the wet grass by this grave. To my horror, as if in some slow-motion film, I felt him lose hold of my leg and my momentum carried me to the very edge of the cliff and over.

I clawed in desperation at the grass. It slipped through my fingers. Despite the thunder and hammering rain, I could hear the sea smashing against the cliff face far below.

I managed to grab hold of one clump of grass but once again it dragged through my fingers. I was falling. The cliff edge was a slope – a very steep slope; if I fell much further it would become a sheer drop. I clawed at the ground, my fingernails tearing at it. My strength left me. I ached all over with the effort. I knew I could hold on no longer.

My fingers went limp and I felt gravity pulling me down over the cliff edge. My feet were hanging over in mid-air, my knees scraping on the rough earth, my useless hands flapping at the soaking ground. My body was heavy, as though it was already dead. I was falling, falling to be lost in the wild sea below.

Then suddenly, strong hands grabbed my wrists. My body juddered to a halt and was hauled back up the steep slope. There was a flash of lightning. In its glare I saw the stupid face of Mr Potato.

16. Caught!

I was dragged through the churchyard and past the porch of St Mary's, where Lisa was still held by the thin man. There was no sign of the vicar.

'Frank! I've got him, Frank!'

'I told you not to use my real name!'

'Sorry, Frank. What shall I call you, Frank?'

'You weren't supposed to call me anything,' said Frank, 'but it's too late now. I think they know my name's Frank.'

'At least they don't know my name's Bernard,' said the other, then slowly realized what he had said.

'Well done!' said Frank crossly. 'Why don't

you tell them your address and telephone number while you're at it!'

'Sorry,' said Bernard.

We were taken to the car. Bernard Potato sat in the back with us, which meant it was very squashed, while Frank drove.

We drove out of the car park and away, past the abbey, down the steep hill that leads back into Whitby, across the New Bridge, and were soon on the main road, the A171, which Mum and Dad and Rachael and I had taken so many times on our way back home. I wished they were all here now. Dad would sort things out. Mum would beat these men up with her handbag.

Then, suddenly, we stopped in a lay-by. No-one was about.

'What happens now?' asked Bernard.

'We'd better blindfold them,' said Frank, 'so they can't see where we're going.'

'Have you got a blindfold?' asked Bernard.

'No. Have you?'

'No.'

'Shut your eyes, kids,' said Frank, 'and no peeping.'

'Yeah, watch it!' said Bernard.

'How can we watch it if we've got our eyes closed?' I asked.

'Just shut up!' said Frank.

We drove on. I kept my eyes shut for a few minutes and then opened them. Bernard didn't seem to notice so I kept them open. Good job. I get car sick if I close my eyes.

We were going across country. I didn't recognize where we were anyway – somewhere on the North York Moors, but they are very big. We could have been anywhere. After what seemed ages we pulled into a big lay-by. There was an ice-cream van at the far end. Too far away to shout for help. Frank got out and walked over. Great. Here I was, cold and wet, and he was getting me an ice cream.

He came back with four ice creams, four packets of crisps and four cans of cola. They were all sort of balanced in his hands and under his arms, two packets of crisps gripped between his teeth. He had so much stuff that he walked funny to avoid dropping it. When he got back to the car he didn't have a spare hand to open the door. He tried to speak but couldn't open his mouth because of the crisps. It sounded like, 'Mm, mm m m!' Which I translated in my head as 'Bernard, open the door!'

I was by the window, so I could see exactly

what was going on. Bernard couldn't and just sat there.

Frank tried louder: ' MM, MM M M!'

Bernard heard him this time. 'What is it, Frank?'

Frank tried again.

'Sorry, Frank, I can't hear you.'

'MMMMMMMMMMMMMM!'

I wasn't sure, but this time I think there were a few extra words – some of them rude. Bernard suddenly seemed to understand and reached across me to open my door. It flung open and hit Frank smack on his leg.

'Ow!' It was like an avalanche. The crisps fell, then the cans and finally one of the ice creams, which landed upside down on his shoe. 'Thank you, Bernard. Thank you very much. When I said "Open the door" I meant *my* door, not *your* door, you big fat fool.'

'Sorry, Frank.'

'You can eat this ice cream on my shoe!' He picked it up. The top was all squashed in and looked a funny colour. His shoe had a white circle of ice cream on it. He got into the car and passed us the crisps and the cola and the ice creams. Salt and vinegar: my least favourite flavour – the crisps, I mean, not the ice cream.

I opened my can of drink. Because it had been dropped it was all fizzy inside and spurted out. I shot Bernard in the eye. He looked cross. He looked even crosser when Lisa shot him in the other eye. But what finally did it was when he opened his own can and shot himself – full in the face. Cola dripped everywhere.

'Nice suntan,' said Frank, laughing, glad to get his own back. Bernard was not amused.

I ate it all, even the crisps. Salt and vinegar ones always make my tongue go funny. Never mind – I washed the taste away with the drink and the ice cream.

Then we caused a bit of an upset. 'I need the toilet,' said Lisa.

'Me too!' I said.

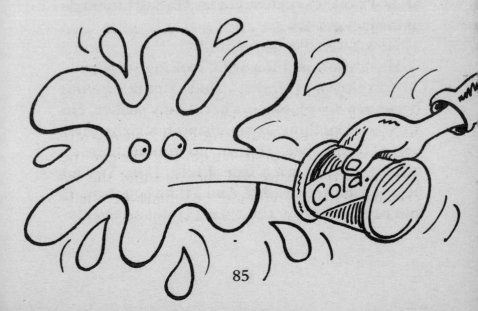

17. Threats

'Right,' said Frank, 'get out.'

We stood by the car with Bernard holding our arms. Frank was in front of us. He had his hands in his jacket pocket.

'Now listen. I've got a gun!'

'Have you?' said Bernard, looking surprised.

'You know I have,' said Frank, giving Bernard a dirty look. 'It's here in my pocket.' He pointed something at us inside his right-hand pocket. 'You two, there's no toilets here so you're going to use a tree. Right, Lisa. You go behind that tree, right? And I'll be counting. If you're not back by the time I count to twenty, your boyfriend here will be looking for a new head.'

'You'll be looking for a new jacket,' I said, 'if you shoot the gun through your pocket.'

'Shut up,' said Frank.

'Can I see the gun?' I asked.

'No.'

'Is it invisible?'

'I said shut up!'

'I don't think you've got a gun,' I said. 'I think you're just pointing your fingers at me. It doesn't even look like a gun.'

'Have you got a gun?' asked Bernard.

'Bernard,' said Frank, sighing, 'you're supposed to be on my side.' He took his hands out of his pockets. There was no gun.

'Lisa,' he said, 'go behind that tree quickly. And no funny business like running for help or Bernard here will sit on Robert's head.'

'Can't you shoot me instead?' I asked.

Lisa ran behind the tree.

'One . . . two . . . three . . .' Frank started counting.

'I'm being as quick as I can!' shouted Lisa.

Frank was still counting: '. . . eight . . . nine . . . ten . . .'

Come on Lisa, I thought. I was looking at

Bernard. He looked just like he sounded – like a bag of potatoes. A big bag. Not something you'd want to sit on your head.

'. . . seventeen . . . eighteen . . . Hurry up, Lisa . . . your boyfriend's got too nice a face to sit on!'

Lisa came running from behind the tree, tucking in her T-shirt. Like me, she was still wet from the rain. 'He's not my boyfriend!'

'OK, boyfriend,' said Frank, 'your turn; but for you I'm going to count quicker.'

'Boyfriend' indeed. I ran behind the tree and tried to go. I was bursting; it should have been easy but I was so scared I couldn't go.

I remember once I had to go in a bottle at the doctor's. I needed the toilet, but somehow as soon as he asked me to do it in a bottle I dried up. The receptionist gave me a drink of water – and then another – but nothing. I was like a desert on legs. Two hours it took. Mum and I went for a walk around the town and I had to go back at the end of surgery time. It was ridiculous. I still don't know why he wanted me to do it in a bottle – why didn't he drink lemonade like everyone else?

Mum said it was nerves that stopped me going then. If it was nerves then, now I was about to have a nervous breakdown. This was serious nerves. Frank was up to number ten. I couldn't do a number one!

I strained and I strained. I thought my eyes were going to pop out. I started to think about running taps, rivers, seas, oceans.

'Hurry up!' shouted Frank. 'Go and see what he's doing, Bernard.'

I could hear Bernard walking towards me. I tried to think of a waterfall. I strained. His footsteps came nearer.

Suddenly the dam burst. The relief was total. Bernard put his hand on my shoulder – I turned and finished off on his foot. He was not amused.

18. Car Journey

Back in the car, Lisa and I sat on either side of Bernard again.

'Thank you very much for the lift,' I said. 'You can take us home now.'

'I'm afraid you're not going home just yet,' said Frank. 'Me and my friend have some unfinished business and we don't want you two in the way.'

'Don't worry about us,' said Lisa. 'We won't get in your way at all. We'll keep right out of your way. I promise.'

'Yes,' I said. 'We'll go to Australia if you like.'

'Sorry,' said Frank. He looked serious. 'But

it's too late for that. You two kids have messed up our plans once and we're going to make sure that doesn't happen again.'

I wanted to look at Lisa but there was a big bag of potatoes in the way: Bernard.

'If you two hadn't been playing in the lifeboat that day, none of this would have happened.'

I agreed with him. I made a promise to myself never to play in a lifeboat again when people were planning a bank robbery outside!

'You wouldn't shut up. We have a job to do – to rob that bank – and we don't want you two stirring things up again, bringing the police in.'

'Well, now they'll know we were right,' I snapped. 'The police won't exactly think we're out shopping. You've kidnapped us!'

'They don't know that,' said Frank. 'All they know is that you've gone missing. Two kids who have already caused the police trouble. Kids who go where they shouldn't go, play in places they're not supposed to play – like lifeboats, for example. And you know, that will help us. They'll be too busy looking for you to bother about watching the bank.' He gave us a stupid smile, started the car and we were on our way again.

The car heater was on and I could feel my

damp clothes steaming. I smelt horrible. I asked Bernard if he'd got any underarm deodorant. He looked at me with an open mouth. He'd never heard of the word. 'I'll buy you a dictionary for Christmas,' I said.

'Shut up,' said Frank.

I must have fallen asleep because I suddenly woke up with a jolt, feeling sick. Every bump and turn in the road made me feel queasy. I wondered what would happen if I *was* sick. I knew I shouldn't have eaten salt and vinegar crisps! I just couldn't get them out of my mind – or rather, out of my mouth. I could taste them. Sooner rather than later I would be seeing them again. Frank wouldn't be the only one with food on his shoe.

I was just about to say something when Frank stopped the car. We had just come over the top of a steep hill. He pulled into the side of the road and yanked on the handbrake. 'Bernard, it's time. The call will be coming through. Pass me the walkie talkie.'

Walkie talkie? I thought. That's the kind of thing a brain-damaged parrot would say.

Bernard pulled a mobile phone out of his jacket pocket. I was trying to think of a joke about a potato wearing a jacket – as in 'jacket potato' – when he nearly had my eye out with his elbow.

Frank took the phone. After a few seconds it rang. He pressed a button and there was a screech of feed-back. It sounded as if whoever was on the other end was screwing up an empty crisp packet in front of the phone. The static was awful. I could just about make out a voice. I also knew why Frank called the phone a 'walkie talkie': whoever it was on the other end sounded just like a brain-damaged parrot.

Then the line went dead. Frank said a rude word.

'Try hitting it,' said Bernard.

'I'll hit you in a minute,' said Frank. 'These things don't work in the car. I'll go over there and try.' He pointed up the hill.

Frank set off, shaking his mobile – obviously trying to get it to work. Perhaps he was trying too hard because the next minute he did a 'Bernard' and fell flat on his face. He'd tripped over a clump of heather.

Bernard waited for Frank to get up. He didn't. And Bernard didn't know what to do. Should he stay with us or go and help Frank? He chose Frank.

Bernard tried to get past me. It was like being

in a cinema. You've just sat down and got comfortable when someone needs to get past. You stand up, your seat stands up too because it's on a spring, and the person squeezes past. No matter how thin they are it's always a struggle. Bernard was fat and it was more than a struggle – it was impossible! The car seat wasn't on a spring. I just sat there getting squashed. In the end he pushed me out, climbed out himself, then pushed me back in. He set off towards the fallen Frank.

'Come on, Robert,' said Lisa. 'Home time.'

We quietly opened our doors and were just about to slip out when I had a brainwave. Frank had left the keys in the ignition. I reached over.

'You're not going to drive, are you?' asked Lisa in a worried whisper.

'No, I haven't passed my driving test.'

All I did was take the keys and, once we were out of the car, throw them as far away as I could into the long grass. It was quite dark. They'd never find them. Once my dad was feeling guilty and decided to be a 'good father' and took us for a game of cricket on the green and his contact lens fell out. We spent hours down on our hands and knees trying to find it. Dad said it was like looking for a needle in a haystack and I said that was a stupid place to look for a needle, Mum's sewing box was better. He didn't think that was funny. We never found it, and the next day they cut the grass so it's now in about a million pieces. We never heard the end of it. Mum nearly killed him. I hoped Frank and Bernard would have the same problem now.

We set off down the hill trying to run on tiptoe, which isn't easy. It's like when you try to creep downstairs at night and you always stand on the stair with a creak! My trainers sounded as if they needed oiling and we both seemed to find all the noisiest twigs to stand on. It was only a matter of time before we were seen or heard.

Frank yelled. Either he'd seen us or Bernard had stood on his toe. We took no chances and broke into a full-speed sprint.

I don't know if you've ever run down a hill and reached that speed where you're going so fast you lose control. Well, that's how fast we were going. We would need a parachute to brake. We didn't have one.

The two men jumped into the car. We could hear their reaction when they saw that the keys were missing. I'm not sure what happened next. I can only guess that Bernard had the idea of catching us in the car even without the keys.

The car was facing down the hill – so he could let off the handbrake and freewheel to us. Bad idea.

I risked a quick look round and saw the car. It was moving fast. Bernard was hunched over the steering wheel, desperately trying to turn it. Frank was waving his arms in the air, panic in his eyes. Suddenly I realized what was happening. Without the keys, the steering wheel was locked. The road was turning to the left but the car was carrying on in a straight line – off the road and into the trees.

Frank shouted something to suggest that Bernard was not the brainiest person who had ever lived. Not in those words. And then there was a thud – presumably the car trying to climb a tree.

This was our big chance to get away.

Mind you, I had something else to worry about. How on earth was I going to stop?

19. Escaping

We were charging down the hill completely out of control. I was running so fast that my body was juddering like a washing machine having a fit. My jaw was wobbling up and down as though it was on a piece of elastic. Fortunately the hill started straightening out and then going up again and we came to a natural stop.

'Get me an oxygen tent – quick,' I wheezed.

We both stood gulping for air like fish out of water, our arms and especially our legs feeling as if they belonged to someone else. My legs were fizzing. It was as if I could feel the blood inside racing around. My ankle hadn't appreciated the strain either. It was reminding me that I had twisted it earlier and it wasn't very pleased.

As we regained control of our lungs, we looked around.

'Where are we?' asked Lisa.

Apart from the obvious fact that we were somewhere in the middle of the North York Moors, I hadn't a clue. That didn't go down too well.

We knew we had to keep moving. Frank and Bernard would be after us, and we needed to find help. If help wouldn't come to us, we had to look for it. We started walking. We had no idea where we were heading, just that we were walking away from you-know-who.

We went cross country – not so much as a short cut, but because we thought Frank and Bernard would probably stick to the roads. The grass was soaking from the rain. Night had somehow come while we weren't looking. The moon kept disappearing behind a cloud.

I don't know how long we walked. We were cold, wet and miserable. We seemed to be walking for ever. My ankle didn't help. It wasn't pouring with blood or anything dramatic; it just ached. It was especially difficult through the scratching heather and wet grass.

'Do you want me to make you a walking stick?' asked Lisa. I ignored her.

Finally, we came out of the trees and back onto a muddy track.

'There's bound to be a house somewhere round here,' said Lisa; 'a farmhouse or something . . .'

'I hope so,' I sulked. 'I'm starving. I could eat a horse!'

'Are you going to have it with chips?' Lisa giggled.

'No, I'll have it in a sandwich with some *horse*radish sauce,' I said. Things couldn't be too bad if I could still make useless jokes.

'We've got to find a proper road,' Lisa said. 'If there's a road, there will be a house.'

'Or even a car!' I suggested. 'We could flag it down and ask for help.'

And so on we went, walking into the night. We were tired but most of all we were hungry, and in a funny way that's what kept us going: comparing what foods we were going to eat when we got home.

Lisa said a horse would be too small and she

would have an elephant burger, so I said I'd have a whale pie, so she said she'd have a dinosaur on toast, etc. etc.

And then we saw it: looming up through the darkness, the clear shape of a house. There were no lights on, but it was a house. And a house meant safety.

Everything was going to be all right.

20. Safe as Houses

The strange thing was that although we were getting closer and closer to the house, it didn't seem to be getting any bigger. In fact, there was definitely something wrong. It was the right shape for a house – it had a roof, a chimney, a door. But it was very small – about the same size as our garage. I wondered if the moonlight was playing tricks with my eyes.

'It's not a house,' said Lisa.

'Well what is it?' I asked. 'A fruit cake?'

'Don't be stupid, Rob!' she snapped. 'It's not a *proper* house. It's a shepherd's hut or something.'

And Lisa was right.

There were thousands of sheep on the North York Moors, and I suppose this was a place where the shepherd could shelter or maybe sleep in during bad weather or lambing. But, being our luck, there was no shepherd in at the moment. We knocked on the door, knocked on the window, shouted through the keyhole. We went round the back. There was one other window there – we knocked on that too.

'There's never a shepherd in when you need one,' I said. 'And I was going to ask him to cook me a shepherd's pie.'

'Very funny,' moaned Lisa. 'What now?'

'We'll just have to try and find a cottage and get some cottage pie.'

We walked back to the front of the house, talking over what we might do: a) we could carry on walking and try to find a proper house, b) we could wait outside until the shepherd turned up – which could be in about ten years' time, or c) we could break in.

We chose c).

I started by kicking the door – I had to use my good foot – then bashed at it with my fists. It didn't budge. I wanted to charge at it like they do in police films, but Lisa had a better idea: 'Why don't we try the handle?'

Lisa took the handle, turned it and opened the door. If my chin hadn't been fastened to my face it would have fallen on the floor.

We went in.

21. Home Comforts

The hut wasn't exactly a luxury hotel. It wasn't even a luxury shepherd's hut. In fact it was a dump! There was no light apart from the moonlight coming in through the windows, and the only furniture was a table and chair and a cupboard that looked as though my dad had built it. There was a mattress on the floor with a blanket, and a fireplace. There was no telephone, so we couldn't ring for help. I went to the cupboard and opened the door, which was so wonky that it nearly came off in my hands.

Inside the cupboard was a packet of biscuits that looked as though it had been there since the Victorians, a candle, a box of matches and a bread knife. No bread!

As it was dark we decided to light the candle, but that was easier said than done. Everything was damp, including the matches, and we wasted most of them: the heads just disintegrated on the side of the box. One match sort of spluttered into half a flame but then went out. Lisa tried drying a match on her T-shirt, but as that was still wet it was a pathetic idea.

I know it seems silly, but somehow this stupid candle not lighting was the final straw. I hadn't cried for years, but I could feel myself on the verge of a boo-hoo now. We had three matches left.

The next match worked. The candle spat and the wick gave a feeble little flame. I was sure it was going to die, but it pulled itself together, and soon the room was filled with a pale yellow light.

That light lit our spirits as well as the room. We both felt better just seeing its warm glow.

'Happy birthday to you,' sang Lisa and pretended to blow the candle out.

We sat on the mattress, even though it was damp, and thought about what to do. 'I think the shepherd's wet the bed!' I said.

We were both frozen to the bone. Even my teeth ached with the cold.

'Let's stay here,' I said. 'We'll rest here tonight and in the morning we can go and look for help.'

Lisa agreed. We hoped that Frank and Bernard would be too busy trying to get their car out of the tree, searching for the keys, wandering the moors looking for us, or sleeping, to bother about the shepherd's hut. In any case, we had stumbled on it by accident. The North York Moors were so huge that there was a good chance − especially in the dark − that they wouldn't see it even if they happened to be searching nearby. If Bernard was in charge of the search we would definitely be safe. He was so stupid he needed a map to find his feet to put his socks on. We were taking a chance, but we were both so tired it was a chance we had to take.

Meanwhile, we *had* to get warm. If we stayed as we were, the shepherd's hut would have two extra items: a fridge and freezer. Lisa was the fridge!

The fireplace had some half-burned sticks in it, but they wouldn't last long. There was no point in going outside for more wood − it was all soaking wet from the rain. We had a look round the hut, hoping the shepherd had a stock of firewood, but no such luck.

'There's only one thing for it,' I said. 'We'll have to set fire to the cupboard!'

'The cupboard?' squealed Lisa. 'You can't set fire to someone's cupboard!'

'Well, it looks like a load of firewood anyway,' I said, 'and this is an emergency. I'm sure the shepherd wouldn't mind if he knew the trouble we were in.'

Lisa looked doubtful.

'I'll tell you what,' I suggested. 'When we're out of here and we get back home, I'll *buy* him a new cupboard. But for now, I'm freezing to death. Say goodbye to the cupboard, it's going on the fire!'

I took the packet of biscuits out and put it on the table. Then I laid the cupboard on its side and, without waiting for Lisa to argue, smashed it to bits. It only took a few minutes. Soon the cupboard was a cupboard no more but a pile of junk! It looked even more like something Dad had built.

I put a handful of the smaller pieces of wood in the fireplace and then ripped the paper wrapper from the packet of biscuits, held this in the flame of the candle and, when it was alight, took it to the wood, using it as a firelighter. The cupboard wood was really dry and lit quite easily – a bit too easily really: I thought my eyebrows were going to melt, but we fed it with larger pieces and it settled down into a nice, comforting fire. Except for the smoke.

'I thought smoke was supposed to go up the chimney,' I said.

'It is,' said Lisa, 'but it's having a walk round the cottage first.'

'Great,' I moaned. 'I escape from Thick and Thicker and now I'm going to die from cupboard smoke. There should be a Government Health Warning: SMOKING THIS CUPBOARD KILLS!'

'Stop complaining,' said Lisa, sounding just like my mum. 'Let's have something to eat!'

'Food!' As soon as Lisa mentioned it, I remembered I was starving to death. We searched the hut again, just in case there was a secret supply of food.

'Perhaps we could catch a sheep!' Lisa joked. 'We could use its wool for a blanket and eat the rest!'

'Perhaps we could catch a sheep, train it, and send it out to get us some fish and chips,' was my best suggestion.

Fortunately for the sheep, there was no sheep to be seen. The only thing to eat was the biscuits. They were ginger biscuits, and they were supposed to be gingery and crisp. They were gingery and soggy! I could wobble one between my fingers like a rubber.

'Mmmm. Tasty,' said Lisa sarcastically.

The truth was, we were so hungry that we'd have eaten anything – soggy or not. I put a biscuit in my mouth. 'Ugghh!' I'd have eaten anything *except* this biscuit. It tasted like the inside of a trainer – rubbery and sweaty. Not that I've ever eaten a trainer! Though looking at my trainers drying off in front of the fire I was tempted to eat one now.

Maybe that's what gave me the idea – seeing my trainers steaming. I went and got the bread knife, speared a biscuit and toasted it on the fire.

I can't pretend they were the best biscuits I've ever tasted, but they tasted better warm than cold, and one or two even went a bit crispy. They had a wet, smoky, burnt sort of taste. 'Just like Mother makes,' I joked. We ate the lot. I could have killed for a drink to wash them down, but no such luck.

We sat on the edge of the mattress. It was my

first chance to think about our visit to the bank, the chase and everything. It was all like one of those bad dreams where you are the central character but everything seems to be happening to someone else. You are in it and not in it at the same time. Unbelievable.

Lisa put the last bits of wood on the fire. The smoke was gradually finding its way up the chimney. Our clothes were still damp, but no longer soaking, and we at least felt warm. We lay down on top of the mattress, not bothered about it being wet. We threw the blanket on top, too tired to talk, and fell into an exhausted sleep.

22. 999

The next morning, very early, I woke shivering. The fire was long dead and my damp clothes were cold and clammy. The blanket was gone. I looked round at Lisa. She was fast asleep with the blanket rolled around her. Charming. No wonder I was frozen.

I got up and jumped up and down a bit to get warm as if I was in a demented keep-fit video. I went outside. The sun had just risen and was struggling to start the day. It wasn't raining.

The landscape of the moors was dark and barren, but in the distance I could see something that we had missed the night before: a road. And where there was a road, there would be houses or cars or telephone boxes.

I went back into the hut. Lisa was sitting up on the mattress with the blanket round her shoulders.

I told her of my discovery and we decided to set off straight away, pausing briefly to say goodbye to our hotel: 'Goodbye hotel!'

'I hope that cupboard wasn't a valuable antique,' I joked, looking at the ashes in the fireplace.

We set off. The walk warmed us up, but it was tough going. The heather was hard to walk through. It was rough and scratchy and the ground beneath it was uneven. Sleeping in damp clothes had not helped. The cold seemed to have penetrated to the marrow in our bones.

'Have you got any anti-freeze?' I asked.

My ankle was not the happiest ankle in the world. It would rather have been lying down asleep than walking about like this, but eventually we made it, and there – about 300 metres down the road – was a telephone box. I couldn't believe it. I wondered if it was a mirage. Perhaps hot ginger biscuits and smoke made your brain go funny. We'd expected a long, hard walk to find help, and here it was just standing there.

Forget how tired and aching we were: at the sight of that telephone box our energy returned. I could have run in the Olympic Games and then done the London Marathon and then run up Mount Everest with a hippopotamus on my back. At the sight of that telephone box my body was ready for anything.

We ran for it as though it was a long-lost friend. If my arms had been long enough I'd have given it a hug and a kiss.

Lisa was smiling as if she'd got a coat hanger in her mouth. It was brilliant. We could ring the police – they'd contact our parents and everything would be fine. We could have dry clothes and lots and lots of food.

We pulled open the door and piled in.

'Have you got any money?' asked Lisa, suddenly looking worried.

'No,' I said, 'but you don't need money to ring the police. Nine, nine, nine is free!' I picked up the phone and then suddenly *I* looked worried.

'What is it?' Lisa asked.

'Nothing!' I said.

'Well get on with it then!'

'No – nothing!' I spat out. 'There's nothing here, no sound, nothing. There's supposed to be a noise when you pick up the phone, a sort of purring.'

Lisa snatched the phone out of my hand and put it to her ear. She banged it. She pulled at the wire. She shouted down it. Nothing! 'Dead!' she said. 'It's dead!'

I tried again. I hit it. I dialled random numbers. I swore at it. As it was dead I even pretended to give it artificial respiration. Nothing. I might just as well have tried to ring the police with my trainer!

And then I heard Lisa's sharp intake of breath. 'Rob, look!'

Above the phone, on the board where they print telephone numbers and information, was a piece of white paper torn from a notepad. This is what it said:

Deer Robert and Lisa,
Wee are afraid the fone is not wurking.
luve from
Bernard and Frank.

They had found us! We had to go, and quick.

But we were not going anywhere. As we turned to leave, we saw Bernard outside. We were trapped.

23. Trapped

Nowhere to go. Nowhere to run. Inside a telephone box with a gigantic bag of potatoes blocking the door.

I tried to push at the door, but it was a waste of time.

Frank was there as well, a little further off, standing by a white transit van. He gave me a little wave and a smile. If I was Popeye, I'd have eaten some spinach, smashed open the telephone box and booted him into space. I wasn't Popeye and I didn't have any spinach – I hate the stuff anyway – so I had to let him off.

Frank came up to the telephone box and

shouted, 'Robert and Lisa, hello. It was kind of you to light a fire in your little house. We'd lost you and the smoke told us exactly where you were.'

Lisa and I exchanged glances. That stupid cupboard!

'I left Bernard here to guard you overnight while I went and picked up this van. For some reason, I couldn't find my car keys. We'd seen this phone box last night and guessed you might stop by. After I'd used it to ring about the car, Bernard here made some adjustments to the wiring just in case you tried to ring for help!'

I'd have liked to make some adjustments to Bernard's wiring.

'Now, we want you both to come for a ride in our van. We were going to take you in a nice, comfortable car, but it's parked halfway up a tree.'

Lisa gave me a look.

'Now, we are going to let you into our van one at a time . . . Lisa first and then you, Robert. Be good. Be quiet. And nothing will happen to you.'

We weren't going to argue.

Bernard opened the door just enough for Lisa to squeeze through. Frank took her to the back of the van and helped her in. Then it was my turn. The two men followed me in, closing the door behind them.

The van had two small back windows, but these had been painted over. The sides of the van were metal with no windows. The driver's cab was a separate compartment. It was like a closed box. No-one could see out or in. There were no seats in the back, but there were four rolled-up carpets on the floor and we sat on them.

'Make yourself comfortable,' said Frank. 'We're going for a little ride.'

'These carpets don't have seat belts,' I said. 'That's dangerous.'

'You'll have to use Bernard as an air bag,' laughed Frank. 'He looks like one.'

Bernard looked hurt; like an air bag with a puncture. He stayed with us in the back while Frank got out. In a few minutes we set off.

We had no idea where we were going.

24. Making a Delivery

Lisa and I sat on one roll of carpet. Bernard sat on another opposite us.

It was our first chance to study him, and his head really did look just like a misshapen potato – one of those potatoes you get with nobbly bits on it. A nobbly bit for his chin, a nobbly bit for his nose. It was weird. I'd have liked to turn him into a mashed potato.

Travelling in the back of the van was not a lot of fun. As it changed speed or turned a corner or went up or down a hill, we were rocked around. Bernard looked as if he was on a spring.

We were driven for what seemed like ages,

though it was hard to tell. With no windows to look through, I had no idea of where we were or where we were heading. When we finally stopped, we could have been down in London or up in Scotland or bang in the middle of nowhere as far as I knew.

If I thought I was going to find out when the van stopped, I was mistaken.

'Stand up!' said Bernard. He stood up himself and banged his head on the roof. 'Ooff!!'

'You ought to wear a crash helmet,' said Lisa.

There was a knock on the door. Frank squeezed in. I tried to peer past him to see where we were, but it was impossible.

'We're going to put you two somewhere safe while we finish our little job,' Frank said. 'You've caused us a lot of trouble so we aren't taking any chances.'

'No,' said Bernard, still rubbing his head.

'We're going to take you inside a nice warm house. When we get back we'll let you out. Now we don't want you to see where you are, and we don't want you to be seen.'

'We've got a plan,' said Bernard.

'Yes,' said Frank. 'We're going to carry these carpets into the house and if anyone sees us, they'll think we're just delivery men.'

'Good plan,' I said, 'but we'll still be in the van.'

'No you won't.' Frank smiled. 'That's the clever bit. You'll be inside the carpets!'

'Yes.' Bernard looked pleased with himself. 'You'll be rolled inside, like the sausage in a sausage roll.'

'I'm not going to be a sausage!' I protested.

'You've got no choice,' said Frank. 'Lie down and we'll roll you up in the carpet. We'll just carry you in, then you can get out.'

'You get in the carpet and we'll carry *you* in,' I suggested, though carrying Bernard would require a crane.

'Look!' Frank snarled, getting angry. 'Lie down!'

'Make me,' I said.

25. Carpet Ride

'Make him lie down, Bernard.'

'How?'

'Use your muscles. Make him.'

Bernard moved towards me, his arms outstretched like a big gorilla. I stepped back. Bernard tripped over one of the carpets, hit his head again, this time on the side of the van – 'Ooff!' – and sprawled on the floor.

'I told you to wear a crash helmet,' said Lisa.

'Well done, Bernard,' said Frank. 'If you want something doing, do it yourself.' He pointed at the floor of the van. 'Lie,' he said.

'OK,' I replied. 'You are a beautiful woman

with four legs and Bernard is really brainy.'

Frank gave me a puzzled look.

'Well, you told me to lie!' I said. 'You're not beautiful, you don't have four legs and Bernard is thick. I was lying.'

For a second I thought Frank was going to hit me. He hit Bernard instead. 'Get up, Bernard. You are about as useless as a pair of rubber scissors. I keep telling you, you're supposed to be on my side.'

Bernard struggled to his feet. He looked dazed. Well, more dazed than he usually did, which isn't saying much. It looked as though he was going to have two nice eggs on his forehead. Egg and potato, lovely.

'Look, you two,' said Frank, 'don't make it difficult for us. We don't want to hurt you, we just want you out of the way inside the house. The less you know the better it will be for you when you see the police. We don't want you seeing where we are. We don't want you being seen. The police still think you've wandered off and got shut in somewhere or lost your way, but if someone sees you with us, we've had it. The only way is to hide you by carrying you inside these carpets.'

'Well, as you put it so nicely . . .' said Lisa, '. . . I won't do it.'

'Please,' Frank implored.

This was ridiculous. Frank and Bernard were supposed to be the big, tough bank robbers; we were supposed to be the feeble kids they'd captured, and yet here they were begging *us* for help. We just weren't scared of them.

If they had wanted to hurt us or use force they would have done it before now. I just felt we were cleverer than them – especially Bernard. If my trainer and Bernard were given a test in school, my trainer would come top. I reckoned we could easily outsmart these two. It was just a question of when.

'If you lie down, I'll give you a sweetie,' suggested Frank.

'I don't take sweets from strangers!' I was feeling really confident. I was in charge. I was better than both these two. All I had to do was tell them to surrender: they would give in, Lisa would call the police, I would be a hero!

Then Bernard brought out his secret weapon. He trod on my foot by mistake, the one with the bad ankle attached.

It was like having an elephant wearing lead

trousers and holding a mountain standing on me. My foot felt as flat as a duck's flipper. I fell over in agony.

'Sorry,' said Bernard.

'Well done,' said Frank. And before I could see if any of my toes had dropped off, he held me down and started rolling me up inside the carpet.

I was rolled over and over. It was horrible. My face was pushed into the carpet pile. It smelt stale. I couldn't move at all. It was like being in a strait-jacket. Not that I've ever been in a strait-jacket, but come to that, up until now I'd never been rolled up inside a carpet.

After a few minutes I was picked up. The carpet, with me in it, was taken a short way, put down, picked up again, taken an even shorter way, then put down once more. I was like Aladdin on his magic carpet but the wrong way round. My head end was tipped much higher than my feet and I got the impression I was being taken up some stairs. I was put down again. Whoever it was carrying me managed to drop the end with my head in it. Fortunately the carpet kept me well padded.

Finally I was pulled and pushed up a ladder

or something and my carpet came to rest – I guessed in the attic.

I seemed to be lying there for ages. There's not much to do inside a carpet. I just lay there wondering if my foot would ever recover. As Bernard had stood on it, I'd probably need a size 456 shoe. I'd have to buy one from a clown shop.

Suddenly something heavy landed on me. I guessed this was Lisa arriving in her carpet.

The next minute my carpet was pushed and pulled around and I was being unrolled. I sprawled out onto some rough floorboards. I blinked in the glare of a bare light bulb that hung from a wire. Lisa was sitting staring at me.

I had been right. We were in an attic.

26. The attic

The attic was just an attic. I mean, it hadn't been converted into a room or a swimming pool or anything. The bit we were sitting in had been boarded, but most of it had been left as bare beams with rolls of fibreglass insulation between them, just like we had in our loft at home. There were some boxes and suitcases and piles of newspaper – the usual attic rubbish. Nothing interesting.

'Welcome to your new home!' said Frank. 'Tonight we're going to leave you locked in here while we pay a little visit to the bank.'

'We'll just get out!' said Lisa.

'No chance. We'll leave someone here to guard you. We have a friend downstairs, you know.'

'You've got a friend? He must be desperate,' said Lisa.

'Watch it!' said Frank. 'There's no need to be rude. Now, to change the subject, do you want something to eat?'

'Yes please,' said Bernard.

'Not you, you fool. Robert and Lisa!'

Lisa and I said we were hungry but definitely not for ice cream.

Frank went to the trap door. He slid it to one side and lowered himself onto a stepladder or something – I couldn't see what. The food must have been there waiting for us – perhaps the 'friend' had brought it – because within seconds he was back again carrying a plastic tray with wrapped, shop-made sandwiches and two tins of cola.

'Tuck in,' said Frank.

'Aren't you going to say grace?' I asked.

Frank ignored my brilliant joke and threw me one packet of sandwiches and the other at Lisa. If I'd been an ace detective – Sherlock String – I would have been able to examine the sandwiches and the packet for clues and decide,

a) where we were, b) how to arrest the crooks, and c) how to escape. The only thing I discovered was that they tasted horrible. Still, they were better than cooked ginger biscuits.

We swallowed the last of the sandwiches and washed them down with the cola. Each mouthful of drink spelt a letter in my mind. 'T', then 'o', followed by an 'i', then 'l', and 'e' and finally another 't'. The word it spelt was: 'toilet'.

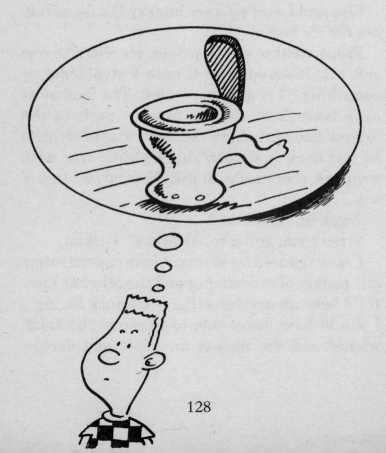

27. Goodbye, Bernard

'I need the toilet,' I said.

'Not again!' said Frank.

'I can't help it. What do you want me to do – build an extension for my bladder?'

'What's a bladder?' asked Bernard.

'*You're* a bladder!' said Frank. 'Go downstairs and ask for a bucket.'

'What for? Have I got to wash the van?'

'No,' explained Frank patiently, 'I want to put the bucket on my head and say "I'm feeling a little pail." Ha Ha.'

Bernard did his potato impersonation again. He didn't understand.

'Go and get a bucket, Bernard. The kids can use it as a toilet.'

'Why can't we use the real toilet?' Lisa asked.

'Because we don't want you to know where you are. Remember?'

Frank opened the trap door and Bernard lowered himself through it. There was a huge crash. 'Someone's moved the ladder!' said Bernard from down below.

After a few minutes he was back, this time using the ladder. He came up into the attic with a red plastic bucket.

'Here we are,' said Frank. 'One portable toilet.'

'I'm not going in that,' said Lisa. 'I'm definitely *not* going in front of anyone else.'

Frank sighed. 'Bernard, take it over there.' He pointed to the far end of the attic. 'We'll try and rig a curtain up or something.'

Bernard picked up the bucket and set off.

'Bernard, be careful. The floorboards don't go all the way. Only stand on the beams. Don't stand between them. The plaster won't hold your weight.'

'I know that,' said Bernard. 'I'm not stupid!'

Unfortunately for Bernard this was not true. He *was* stupid.

He put the bucket on one of the beams, and turned to come back. Being a fat man, tight-rope walking on attic beams was not exactly easy. Somehow he managed to get his legs in a knot. You could see he was losing his balance. He waved his arms around like an ostrich trying to take off, desperately trying to keep his feet on the beam.

But it was no good. Gravity won. He slipped off the beam and stood for a second on the fibreglass insulation that covered the thin plasterboard. He gave Frank a weak smile and a little wave as the plaster split beneath his weight. It sounded like an earthquake, a volcano erupting and an explosion rolled into one.

Bernard fell through the attic floor.

28. Goodbye, Frank

When I say Bernard fell through the attic floor
that is only half true. What I mean is, only half
of him fell through: his legs. When it got to his
stomach, there was a bit of a problem. He was
too fat. He was wedged between two beams with
his legs dangling in mid-air.

'Bernard! You fool!' sighed Frank. 'Get up!'

'I can't. I'm stuck.'

Frank tutted, sighed and went over to the top
half of Bernard. He pulled and pulled. His face
went very red, but Bernard was stuck. 'I'll have
to get some help,' he said. 'Stay there.'

Bernard didn't have any choice.

Frank opened the trap door a little way. Obviously the friend downstairs was there – probably having heard Bernard's attempt to redecorate the ceiling. In fact he *must* have heard – even a stone-deaf stone with ear plugs in must have heard. Frank was talking to whoever it was, but I couldn't hear anything. However, it was obvious they had a plan: get Bernard out! Frank above and the friend below pulling and pushing together.

There's a Laurel and Hardy film where Hardy has fallen through the floor and Laurel tries to pull him out by grabbing his head. All he succeeds in doing is stretching Hardy's neck as long as a giraffe's then letting it go like a piece of elastic. It looked as though Frank was trying the same thing on Bernard.

'Ow. That hurts!'

'Bad luck. It's all your own fault! Falling through the floor!'

The men were so busy, I wondered if we could sneak our way out and escape, but before I had a chance to do anything there was a huge crash.

I don't know quite what happened, but one second Bernard was there, the next he disappeared through the hole, taking Frank with him. The friend down below must have given an extra big pull, the plaster collapsed and Frank fallen off balance – all at the same time.

Lisa and I walked from beam to beam to look through the big hole. What we saw was a real surprise.

29. Flat Out

There was a mess of bodies, arms and legs everywhere, covered with bits of plasterboard, fibreglass insulation and grey dust. Frank was on top, Bernard the filling in the sandwich, and the 'friend' underneath it all, face down, groaning. I can't say I blamed him. Bernard had trodden on my foot and that was heavy enough. Frank and Bernard together squashing you would hurt a million times worse – as well as turning you into a pancake!

Frank rolled off. Bernard rolled off. A very crumpled body in a very crumpled suit lay there, flat out in both senses.

And then I knew.

I had seen that suit before. It was crumpled even before Frank and Bernard had landed. I remembered thinking how that suit needed pressing and how its owner always had his hands in his pockets. It was Mr Seymour – the bank manager. The man whose bank was going to be robbed.

Mr Seymour was lying with his arms and legs out like a big cross, his hands spread out lifelessly. And there I could see it – the final clue. His thumbnail. Not just an ordinary thumbnail, but one that looked as if it had been hit with a hammer, a nail which was a blacky, purply, yellow colour. It was all falling into place. Sherlock String was on the case. Mr Seymour was the third man from the Lifeboat Museum. He was going to rob his own bank.

Lisa and I decided to leg it.

Lisa pulled back the trap door and lowered herself onto the stepladder. I followed. But the way out was blocked by a huge obstruction – Frank and Bernard.

30. Squashed

'And where do you think you're going?' asked Frank.

'We're going shopping,' I said. 'We'll be back in a minute.'

'You're not going anywhere. Stand still. Bernard, look after Seymour.'

Bernard walked past us and bent down by the prone body of the bank manager. 'What happens if he's dead?' he asked in a really worried voice.

'You'll have to bury him!' said Frank. 'But I don't think he'll be very pleased: he's still breathing.'

'At least he's saved from Bernard giving him the kiss of life!' I said to Lisa. 'That would be enough to kill anyone.'

Bernard helped Mr Seymour to turn over and sit up. He looked terrible.

'Go and get a glass of water,' said Frank.

'I'm not thirsty,' said Bernard.

'Not for you, for Seymour! Give me strength!'

Bernard returned and gave Mr Seymour a drink. That seemed to revive him a bit. He looked up at us.

'Are you all right?' asked Bernard.

'It's half past Wednesday,' said Mr Seymour.

'Great!' said Frank. 'He was going to guard these two. He doesn't even know where he is.'

'But this is his house,' said Bernard.

'Well done, Bernard. You've done it again. This is supposed to be a top secret location and you've told them it's Seymour's house.'

'Sorry,' said Bernard glumly.

'It's too late now.' Frank turned to Mr Seymour, whose eyes were going round and round like a spin drier. He held up his hand in front of the bank manager's face. 'How many fingers am I holding up?'

Mr Seymour looked puzzled. 'I don't like sprouts,' he said, and burst out crying.

138

'You don't have to eat any sprouts,' said Frank. 'Give me strength. I think we must have flattened his brain when we landed on him.'

He ordered Bernard to half drag, half lift the semi-conscious man into a bedroom. 'We'll just have to wait and see if he recovers. If not we'll have to take Robert and Lisa with us to the bank. Seymour's made sure the alarms are off. He's altered the time switch so we don't need him to help us at that end. In the meantime, these two might as well use the toilet and then we'll all go downstairs and watch television until it's time to go.'

'Is all this part of your plan?' I asked.

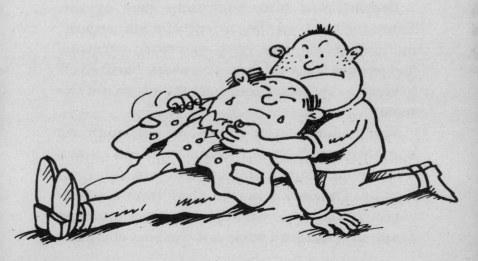

31. A Bank to Rob

We watched television.

Bernard was into Australian soap operas. There seemed to be a continuous supply, including some from years ago when everyone had permed hair and flared trousers. I drifted off to sleep a few times, and I am sure Lisa did the same.

The curtains were drawn, so although we knew this was Seymour's house we didn't know where that was. I guessed not too far from Whitby. The darkness, the glare from the television, the fact that we were very tired, and that Frank and Bernard were not the best company meant that sleep was very easy. Somehow all the soap operas started to muddle into one and I couldn't remember if Charlene was a doctor or a vet or a prisoner or a schoolgirl. I just drifted in and out of Australian dreams.

We should really have been able to escape then – by hitting the men on the head or locking them in a cupboard or something. It sounds easy. Two men with one brain cell between them. My only excuse is that we were very tired and they were very big. Up until now they'd been very nice to us – well, as nice as people who kidnap you could be – but I didn't fancy testing this out. After all, they were the baddies. I'd seen what they'd done to Mr Seymour.

They wouldn't let us talk to each other either, so we couldn't make a joint plan. We were sitting on the settee, Bernard between us. I couldn't even see Lisa properly with a wall of stomach in the way.

We had more sandwiches and cola and were allowed supervised visits to the toilet.

I must have fallen into a deep sleep again. I thought I was in an Australian café having a drink with a kangaroo with permed hair and flared trousers. I remember being really worried that it had an extra trouser leg for its tail and that too was flared – the trouser leg I mean, not the tail. The last thing I saw was a baby kangaroo – a joey – sticking its head out of the trouser pocket, and it also had permed hair. I think I was laughing in my sleep – anyway, the next thing I knew, Frank was shaking me.

'Robert, wake up. It's time. We're going to rob the bank!'

32. The Crime of the Century

I opened my eyes. Lisa was standing with the two men waiting for me. Mr Seymour was apparently still asleep. When Frank had woken him, Mr Seymour had said 'Happy Christmas' and gone off again. They decided to leave him where he was.

We had no-one to guard us, so we were going too.

We went through the kitchen, into the garage, then straight into the van, so we still couldn't see where we were.

Frank drove while Bernard looked after us.

'Why don't you just let us go?' asked Lisa.

'We'll tell the police that you were kind to us.'

'Sorry,' said Bernard. 'We'll let you go as soon as we've robbed the bank, which will be soon. Till then you stay with us. Frank's made me promise.'

Lisa tried her best I-am-a-lovely-person-so-please-let-me-go voice: 'Please.'

'I can't,' said Bernard. 'I've promised Frank. Anyway, I need the money. Sit still. It won't be long.'

We drove for a short while and stopped. Frank climbed into the back. He had a pile of empty sacks with him. 'This is no time for a sack race,' I joked. I was ignored.

'Right, you two, I'm going to stay and guard you while Bernard here opens the bank up. Once he's done that we'll all go inside and you can watch two true professionals at work.'

Frank gave Bernard a bunch of keys. Five minutes later he was back. 'Frank, I can't get in. The keys don't work.'

'Brilliant! Give me strength. The crime of the century, the greatest bank robbery of all time and we can't even get in the front door. Come on, we'll all try.'

We were helped out. The van had been parked outside Woolworths, just a little way from the bank. When we arrived at the door, we saw three keyholes. Frank put the keys in each lock in turn. They opened easily. 'Well done, Bernard. What did you do? Use the keys upside down?'

'Sorry,' said Bernard.

We went in.

Frank typed in some numbers on a little control panel next to a door. He turned the handle and we went through. There was a flight of stairs going down. At the bottom was what looked like the sort of door you get in prisons – certainly prisons in Australian soap operas – a door made of metal bars. Frank had another key for this.

In front of us was the giant metal safe.

There were two more control pads on this with numbered buttons. Frank took a piece of paper from his trouser pocket. It obviously had some kind of code on it because he referred to it as he punched in the numbers. 'Open sesame!' he said. 'Bernard, earn your pay, open the door.'

Bernard pulled at the solid metal door and it swung open.

'Right, Bernard, go inside, turn the light on and start loading the money into the sacks.' He gave Bernard the sacks and turned back to us. 'Right, you two, you can sit down and relax.

We'll load up the money, then we're off. The police will find you here in the morning, by which time we'll be long gone, and everyone will live happily ever after. Amen.'

The words 'don't speak too soon' would have been quite appropriate.

Later, we found out that Bernard had been fumbling for a light switch in the dark safe, but had found the emergency alarm button instead. Not a good idea really. It linked straight to the police station and meant that they would be on their way. The other problem, especially for Bernard, was that it automatically shut the safe door with Bernard locked inside.

'Brilliant!' said Frank. 'Give me strength. We come here to rob a bank and Bernard's locked himself in the safe.'

He tried desperately to open the door. He looked at his piece of paper and punched in various numbers with increasing desperation, but it didn't work. Some sort of security device was in operation. He tried pulling at the handle and went red in the face. He kicked the door and hurt his foot. It was all a waste of time.

He was still trying to get in – whether for Bernard or the money I don't know – when the police arrived.

33. The Master Criminals

Sergeant Jenkins led the police in. There seemed to be loads of them. He obviously knew Frank. 'Hello, Frank. Why don't you use the cash machine like everyone else?'

Frank just looked very, very deflated – like I do when Mum says I have to go to bed just before the best ever programme in the entire history of television comes on.

'Where's Bernard?'

'Locked in the safe!' I said.

Sergeant Jenkins burst out laughing. 'Good one, Bernard. At least he can't get into trouble in there.'

Frank was handcuffed, and a policeman was told to find someone to let Bernard out.

'They'll need a big tin opener,' I suggested.

The sergeant made us tell him everything that had happened. When we got to the bit with Mr Seymour he nodded as though he had half expected it. Two officers were despatched to arrest him.

Someone must have informed our parents because soon they arrived. Our mums burst into tears and hugged and kissed us and kept touching us, almost as if they couldn't believe we were real. Everyone tried to talk at once. Dad sort of jumped up and down, pleased to see me but wanting to get his hands on Bernard. He couldn't get at Frank because by now he was at the police station. Rachael seemed more interested in what the safe looked like! Charming.

Mr Possett arrived his usual cheerful self, with his face looking like a pizza that had been left out in the rain. He typed in some numbers and the safe door opened. He didn't even say thank you to us! Charming!

Bernard came out looking as if he had overslept for about ten years. He looked awful – grey-faced, sweaty and fed up. Two police officers arrested him. He was taken up the steps.

Being Bernard, he managed to trip over Mr Possett's briefcase and he and Mr Possett ended up in a big heap, with Mr Possett underneath. Thanks Bernard, I thought. I couldn't have done better myself!

'Careful, Bernard,' said the sergeant. Dad was smiling too. He realized there was no need for him to beat Bernard up. Bernard was beating himself up and didn't need any help.

'That's why Bernard's brain doesn't work very well,' I said; 'he keeps dropping it!'

I had this brilliant idea for a song called 'Braindrops Keep Falling on My Head', but Mum and Dad and Lisa's mum wanted to get us home as quickly as possible.

34. Loose Ends

We went back to our holiday cottages. Miss Cake was there, and Dad was right about her 'barks and her bites' because she was really pleased to see us and so proud of what we had done that she offered to make us all a lovely hot cup of cocoa. Mum diplomatically got rid of her. I was sent straight to bed with a hot water bottle. I suggested it could be filled with cocoa but Mum thought that was a bad idea.

The next day a doctor came to see me. I had a bit of a cold – probably all that hanging around in damp clothes – and my ankle was a bit swollen. That was just an excuse really: Mum wanted me checked out.

The doctor was from Whitby and looked as though he had been born when dinosaurs ruled the world. He was also one of those adults who don't have a clue how to talk to children. He certainly didn't understand my jokes.

For example, he looked in my throat and said, 'Well, well.'

'No, ill, ill,' I said. 'If I was well I wouldn't need a doctor!'

He gave me a dirty look and peered into my ear. 'Nothing there.'

'What's happened to my brain?'

Mum told me to shut up, but she had that look on her face that meant she was glad I was feeling OK. The doctor left to go and visit Lisa. I hoped she would think of some good doctor jokes herself.

She must have been fine because that afternoon Sergeant Jenkins came round to see us all and he brought Lisa and her mum. We all gathered in our living room.

The sergeant was there to tie up all the loose ends.

Frank and Bernard were locked away and

would face trial for various things like trying to rob a bank, kidnapping sweet innocent children and impersonating potatoes. Mr Seymour was also under arrest.

Apparently, Mr Seymour was a gambler. He played cards for money – big money – and he lost. He had lost a fortune, and all to the same man.

He had been given a month to pay, and Frank and Bernard were the men sent round to make sure he settled up. They were supposed to threaten him but not hurt him. Frank and Bernard were not violent.

Apparently, while they were talking Mr Seymour's contact lens had dropped out and Bernard was helping him to find it. He trod on Seymour's thumb. That's how the thumbnail was bruised and went black.

Seymour knew he couldn't pay. He just didn't have the money. But he knew a bank that did: his bank.

He hit on a plan. He persuaded Frank and Bernard that they would get the money, *plus* much more for themselves, if they robbed his bank. He would give them all the inside information they needed on security, etc., and a set of keys plus the code to open the safe. Once the money was out, Frank and Bernard would have their share, Mr Seymour could pay off his debts and then run away and go and live on a desert island or something.

As it happened, the bank were already concerned about Seymour. There was a suspicion that he had already borrowed some money to pay off earlier debts by 'inventing' a customer to lend to – really himself.

Mr Possett was sent from head office to investigate. Mr Seymour thought he was just a new counter clerk, but he was really a fraud investigator. He was there to keep an eye on Seymour. So much for Sherlock String ace detective: I'd had Mr Possett down as the baddie.

Dad was getting agitated: 'If the bank suspected Seymour was a crook, why didn't they believe Robert and Lisa about the robbery?'

'Good question, sir,' said Sergeant Jenkins. 'They suspected Seymour of fraud, but knew nothing to suggest he might rob the bank. In fact Mr Possett was certain Robert and Lisa were just messing about, wasting our time. He was most worried that the police involvement might stop Seymour dipping into the till before the bank had sufficient evidence to prosecute. He wanted the kids to shut up and go away as much as Seymour.

'As it was, Mr Possett was so busy trying to prevent a small crime, he almost missed a far bigger one.

'Seymour had Frank and Bernard on standby, ready to take Robert and Lisa out of harm's way. He gave them one last chance to back down when they visited him at the bank. When they wouldn't, he rang Frank with a pre-arranged signal, and the rest you know.'

Anyway, thanks to us, and no thanks to Mr Possett, the plan didn't work out. I felt the word 'reward' forming in my mind.

35. The Cocoa Cup Final

And that's really the end. Lisa and I were told that the bank *was* going to give us a reward. It was like winning the Lottery. I could buy myself a television, video recorder, computer, Rolls-Royce, five million packets of chewing gum. I could even buy the shepherd a new cupboard! Except our reward turned out to be a glass elephant each. They weren't even engraved with our names. They said: NATIONAL MIDWAY BANK. YOU'RE NEVER ALONE WITH A NAT MID LOAN. Brilliant. The shepherd would have to buy himself a new cupboard.

If I could have looked into the future, I would

have seen myself putting that elephant on one of the bedroom shelves Dad had made me, the shelf collapsing and the elephant smashing! So my reward turned out to be a glass jigsaw puzzle. I tried to put it back together, but it was impossible, so I threw it in the bin. Some reward!

We finished off our holiday doing very ordinary holiday things like mucking about on the beach. It was great. We even had the Whitby Cup Final. Me, Lisa and Rachael versus Mum, Dad and Lisa's mum. Dad kept showing off and tackling his own team so he could take all the shots at goal. He was pretending to be a commentator at the same time, saying things like: 'Barnet's new centre forward, Matthew String, is the greatest footballer in the universe!'

Unfortunately for Dad, his next shot hit Lisa's mum smack in the stomach. As Dad's team were losing 10–nil, I told her she should take a free kick, which she did. She took a really long run-up and booted the ball straight at the goal. It shot through the air like a guided missile. The goalie leapt and fell full stretch on top of Miss Cake's flower bed, squashing the flowers flat.

I thought we would all be dead. Lisa's mum

turned pale. Dad stifled a laugh and Mum went to help the goalie up.

'Don't worry about a few flowers,' said Miss Cake, ace goalkeeper. 'They'll soon grow again.' She picked the ball out of the mangled blooms and gave it a big kick. I couldn't believe it. Just because we'd been kidnapped and saved a bank from being robbed and helped to catch the bank robbers. 'You can't judge a book by its cover' – as my dad would say.

I said we would have to rename our game the Whitby Cocoa Cup Final.

Despite having the greatest centre forward in the universe, Barnet lost. With Lisa on our side we won easily, even though the third member of our team was more interested in doing cartwheels.

But all good things come to an end, and soon it was time for us to go home.

Lisa and her mum lived in York, which was quite near us. Mum and Dad were keen to keep in touch with Lisa's mum. If you support Barnet you need all the friends you can get!

To be honest, I knew I was going to miss Lisa. I hadn't expected much when I first met her. In fact, had I known she was a girl I wouldn't have bothered. That would have been my problem:

she had proved herself a real friend, whatever anyone at school might say.

When it was time for the String family to drive off, everyone hugged and kissed. Even Miss Cake gave Mum and Dad a kiss. I couldn't believe it. For one horrific minute I thought I would be her next victim. Aaagh! I managed to move away and go over to where Lisa was standing. We just looked at each other – that was enough. I could read the friendship in her eyes. She could see the same in mine.

And soon there I was, back in the car driving home, Mum and Dad's Sixties tape blaring out.

I looked out of the window and thought back over my holiday. I wondered if Miss Cake would be brewing herself a vat of cocoa or practising her goal kicks. I wondered how Mr Seymour would be feeling in prison and how Frank and Bernard were. Whether Bernard had locked himself in the prison toilet, whether the prison uniform included a crash helmet for when he bashed himself on the head! I wondered if he had squashed anybody yet. He had squashed my foot, Mr Seymour and Mr Possett. I felt very sorry for anyone sharing a cell with him, especially if it was Frank.

It was certainly a holiday I would never

forget. The worst ever and the best ever, all thanks to Lisa Peak, the unlucky charm.

Robert String and Lisa Peak. Not quite the Famous Five. Even if you included Rachael we were just the Famous Two and a Half. But we had made a great team.

Somehow, I just knew, we had many more adventures still to come.

THE END

KNOT AGAIN!

Mike Smit

Robert String – no *ropey* jokes about his name please – is on holiday again with his footballing friend Lisa

Robert and Lisa have been warned to stay out of trouble but then they spot a tall stranger trying to break into their caravan . . . And he bears a distinct resemblance to the Masked Warrior, the wrestler they've just seen in a show. They are determined to make him the *un*Masked Warrior, but they are not helped by a forgetful holiday rep called Carol, a peculiarly kind wrestler called Vivian Vivian and crateloads of corny jokes . . . *Oh no, KNOT AGAIN!*

From the author of *All Tied Up*, another Robert String mystery.

0 440 863732

CORGI YEARLING BOOKS